The Chameleon House

The Chameleon House

short stories

Melissa de Villiers

modjaji books

Published in 2015 by Modjaji Books

PO Box 385, Athlone, 7760, Cape Town, South Africa

www.modjajibooks.co.za

© 2015

Edited by Andie Miller

Cover artwork by Carl Becker

Cover lettering by Jesse Breytenbach

Book layout by Andy Thesen

Printed and bound by Megadigital, Cape Town

ISBN 978-1-920590-89-5

Ebook ISBN 978-1-928215-01-1

To my father and mother:
Andre Rex Wepener de Villiers
Nova de Villiers, née Bezuidenhout

Contents

We look at the world once, in childhood.
The rest is memory.
— Louise Glück, *Nostos*

There are some things one remembers even
though they may never have happened.
— Harold Pinter, *Old Times*

A Letter to Bianca

The old men running the apartheid regime finally threw up their hands and declared a state of emergency in 1985. By this time, my own emergency was already well underway. I had no qualifications and not a cent to my name, and a tormenting problem stood in the way of me acquiring any. I wanted to be a writer, although I hadn't the courage to tell anyone just yet. The reason was simple: whenever I put pen to paper, the words evaporated. Deep in the dark root of me, something writhed and would not sit still. I couldn't shake the queasy conviction that I had nothing original to say.

My father, tired of paying for university courses I wasn't managing to finish, found me a six-week internship on the *Baviaan's Drift Bugle*. I would be given board and lodging by Mr Ossendryver, an accountancy teacher. My father knew him from his own, far-off student days in a Boland town. They'd drunk beer and played rugby together, and it was there that the two of them first heeded bookkeeping's siren call.

I have no idea why I agreed to this miserable venture. I didn't want to leave the city for some godforsaken dorp in the middle of the Eastern Cape. Anyway, did desk jobs matter when a revolution was just around the bend? Anyone could see it was a touchpaper time, when to fuss over career prospects seemed at best, naïve; at worst, contemptible. There were stands to be taken, institutions to be overthrown. At parties in student flats, in city bars and back bedrooms, opinions flew from my lips in a jittery stream. I was nineteen-and-a-half years old.

My father listened to my tirades with bowed head, gently swirling the ice in his glass of gin. One bright blue morning in early spring, he drove me to Johannesburg's Park Station, pressed fifty rand into the pocket of my Indian print skirt and kissed me on the forehead. My tour of the provinces had begun.

Twenty-two hours later, my near-empty bus arrived in Baviaan's Drift; I was the only passenger to alight. A dawn breeze dried the sweat on my trembling hands. Mr Ossendryver, tall and owlish, with small, round glasses and a grey moustache, collected me from the station and took me to his home, an unappealing bungalow on Vermeulen Street.

The house looked small from the outside, but was oddly capacious, with crooked steps leading down to one narrow room after another, stretching out so far ahead that it resembled a railway carriage shunted onto a dead-end track. My room had a window scarcely larger than an envelope, through which a dreary half-light fell. Somehow, it came as no great surprise to find that the back yard overlooked a cemetery. All that stood between the tombstones and me was a solitary outbuilding – the maid's quarters, as it turned out – that cleaved to Mr Ossendryver's back wall.

Mr Ossendryver and I ate together every evening. It was always hot in the dining room, so hot you couldn't breathe. Everything would be sinking sleepily into the big, silent house until suddenly there was Leocardia clearing away the plates and Mr Ossendryver leaning back in his chair and lighting his pipe, and continuing with renewed vigour to pour out the story of his life in smoky, spiralling plumes: the death of Annalie, his wife, from a dog bite that went septic; his years of service at the high school, burdened with ungrateful students who did not wish to learn; the trials, living so far from the city, of keeping up to date with accounting trends; his struggles with athlete's foot and the doctor's advice. I just stared at the salt-and-pepper set, crushing the tips of my hair between two fingers and marvelling at the mess I'd made of things. Around nine, he'd leave the room with a copy of *National Geographic* tucked under his arm and I would know – with my gruesome new field awareness of all things Ossendryverish – that he was headed for a lengthy session in what he called 'the lav'.

Those years were a time of bewilderbees. The country was filled with a strange vibration; it shook like the skin of a drum. Mass rallies, murderous secret police, torture, bombs and jail – all these pulsed louder now into ordinary life, changing the centre of gravity, wrenching everything towards a rhythm that was unpredictable and new. The whole world heard it, and the *Baviaan's Drift Bugle* heard it too, but only faintly. The paper stood aloof from change; it was saving its voice for a more urgent occasion. I understood all this several days later than I should have done. Maybe I was disconcerted at first by how high the *Bugle* ranked itself in the scheme of things, a swan in muddy waters. Maybe I was just unusually self-absorbed.

The paper occupied a thick-walled, Frontier War-era building with lacy fretwork balconies, set back from the broad main road. In the newsroom, rock-faced farmer's sons with deep golf tans pored over stories about drunk driving arrests and pothole repairs, or sped off in their Ford Cortinas to report on rugby games. My first mission as one of their number was to visit the town's lone hardware store and purchase a padlock. The editor – an old man with tinted lenses and a thin, disgusted smile – told me it was for the office stationery cupboard; he didn't want people to think they could just 'help themselves' to the *Bugle*'s notepads and ballpoint pens any more and give them out as Christmas presents. Rumour had it that he was a Special Branch spy.

What to make of it all? Nothing manageable. I knew, at heart, that the situation was profoundly serious but it also just seemed absurd. Anyway, I was too tired to think about anything much. Every night, a sense of unease came to find me, a dark strobe that beamed out anxiety and wouldn't let go till morning. Shifting about in Mr Ossendryver's narrow spare bed, searching for some cave in which to take cover, I'd drift through the night in a fuzzy wasteland of panic and bad dreams. I tried going to bed earlier, but it didn't help. Sometimes, in my enervated state, the room with its homely furniture would seem to grow strange and magical, filled with discarded alien implements that were beyond all human ken. I'd rise and pace about before a glimpse of Mr Ossendryver on the back stoep brought me down to earth in an instant, the very banality of the scene – pipe; tobacco pouch; patio chair; him gazing vacantly out towards Leocardia's shed – locking me back inside a reality apparently so temperamental that all traces had nearly disappeared.

One morning, unable to bear the thought of drifting through another work day on a wash of tedium and fatigue, I decided to call in sick. I rolled a sizeable joint – the last of my stash from the city – and smoked it, brazenly, in bed, beneath an agitated fan. Outside, blossom covered Baviaan's Drift in a white stupor. I felt like I was the last person left standing in a lunar landscape, and it was only a quarter to ten.

It was time to find human company, so through the dark, stuffy house, full of combative chair legs, I dragged my aching frame. Leocardia was in the kitchen feeding Baxter, a big ginger tom with a magnificent gossamer tail. He lived at an elderly neighbour's but much preferred Leocardia, she of the plump, soft lap; Leocardia, who was equally indifferent to newcomers from the city and who viewed the world with the same impenetrable golden gaze.

After a moment or two, she returned to her ironing. Deftly, her small, fine-boned hands soothed the iron's hissing muzzle with pliant folds of cloth, her eyes with their yellowish whites occasionally glancing my way. I planted myself at the table, in the middle of her kingdom, and slowly opened my book. Leocardia never said a word. I was reading *The Great Gatsby*, and when I got to the scene where the young narrator's relatives ponder his future with grave and hesitant faces – finally saying 'Well, ye-es' to him taking a job in New York – the indignity of my own, summary banishment to the countryside stabbed at me anew. I read on, the words and sentences slowly filling me with a pleasure that was almost painful: everything, the iron's hiss, the cat's purr, Leocardia's yellow glance, grew extraordinarily sharp and still. I stared, rooted, at the floor, unable even to lift a hand to scratch my cheek, yet desperate to run away.

A rap at the back door affronted Baxter and shattered the spell. At that moment, I hated the caller who stood on the threshold, even though I'd never seen him before: a burly man with greying hair, wearing faded blue overalls that smelled of smoke. His eyes raked Leocardia over; regally, she inclined her head. His forehead was stippled with sweat, even though it was cool outside. Leocardia stood upright with her arms folded, her legs like two pillars planted far apart. The conversation – in isiXhosa, which I didn't understand – was as brief as it was baffling. Suddenly, she swivelled on her heel and clicked the door shut. The man's eyes had never left her face.

Leocardia threw me a strange look before burying her features in one of Mr Ossendryver's freshly ironed pinstriped shirts. 'He's my brother, that one,' she said, or I thought she said through the folds. 'He doesn't like me living here.' But by then I'd found the thread of my book again, and so it did not occur to me until later, when Mr Ossendryver came home to a cold stove, and Leocardia's room locked and dark, to ask myself if I had heard her right; why she had spoken to her relative so miserably in her low, gruff voice, or why he had thrown out so many angry-sounding questions, to which there had been just as many fierce replies.

Mr Ossendryver took me to Steers steakhouse for a substitute dinner of burgers with avocado and bacon and chips with tomato sauce. To begin with, both of us ate in silence. But when he had patted his moustache with a handkerchief and called for the bill, he started talking as usual about the limitations of small town life. We began the short walk back up the main road to Vermeulen Street, his precise, breathy tones never faltering.

When we reached the big jacaranda by the petrol station he stopped and abruptly cleared his throat. 'She's at Nyami's,' he said.

I looked at him. 'Excuse me?'

'Nyami, the maid where Baxter lives. The note said. Ja, Leocardia and her are great pals, always popping back and forth between the houses with some little joke or other, or an interesting titbit to share about their day.'

'Uh-huh,' I said.

'A remarkable woman, Leocardia,' he went on. 'Lived in this area all her life, although her father's people, I gather, come from somewhere near Addo. You've been to the elephant park there?'

'No, I never have.'

'Oh, you should,' he said. 'What they're doing for the wildlife there is outstanding. It's only a three-hour drive. You know, when I feel under pressure about things, it's the place I like to go. I just throw a few things on the back seat of the car and I set off for Addo with a packet of biltong for the road. Or sometimes tennis biscuits.'

'Lovely,' I said, grinding the ends of my ponytail almost to powder between a finger and thumb.

'I take plenty of snaps and when I get them back from the chemist I show them first to Leocardia,' said Mr Ossendryver. 'We sit at the kitchen table after I've washed up the plates, and she spreads them all out in a row. We spend hours looking at the pictures together, drinking a beer or two and listening to jazz on the wireless. She likes the smaller things; the birds. The Greater Double-Collared

Sunbird, that's her favourite. I want to take her there someday. When it's allowed.'

When it's allowed. On the horizon, I could see a long line of purplish clouds patrolling the valley rim. It was getting late, the shadows lengthening into night. Earlier, I'd opened a letter from Bianca, one of my closest friends. How's life on the sheep station? she asked. Describe it to me, you must have so many stories; and I ached to begin at once, as if completing this simple task was the key to allowing life to finally declare itself to me and set out its demands. But I could not, the old fear again asserting itself: not enough dazzle, not enough flair.

The Friday before, in the bar of the Balmoral Hotel, the staff photographer asked if I'd ever had any literary aspirations. He and I had been covering a story on the far side of town, where a woman who took in student lodgers from the African Theological College found her cat swinging from the doorway by its caked and seeping tail. YOU WHO WALK WITH THE BLACK NATION BEWARE, someone had squirted round the frame.

The staff photographer was a Scot; short and compact, with grey hair closely shorn around a face that was as pale and smooth-shaven as a stone. He had a blunt sense of humour that could be lethal, yet it was not unattractive. The *Bugle* rated his work highly. It was a mystery, most people said, why he hung around in the sticks when he could so easily have found a post on one of the nationals.

'Me, a writer? No. No, not at all,' I replied.

'No?' he persisted. 'Every journalist I've ever met thinks they have a novel inside of them. But you're not tempted? Not even the one little short story fluttering within?'

There was a silence that seemed to have been there a long time, waiting for me. I pictured throwing in my lot with the *Bugle* and settling down in Baviaan's Drift forever. Perhaps I could become one of its 'characters', trailing ropes of ethnic jewellery, reciting weepy poetry to other people's husbands in parked cars late at night.

'And you?' I said, eventually. 'Would you ever exhibit your work? You could show the rest of the country the truth about the unrest in the Eastern Cape.'

'Ah, *the truth*!' he said, with a quick, delighted sneer; too late, I could have bitten off my tongue. 'That's far too complicated a notion for my poor brain to wrestle with. No, I'm a take-it-or-leave-it, point-and-shoot kind of guy; I leave *the truth* up to the romantics. To people like you.'

He wiped his palms down the sides of his jeans, picked up his camera and took a photograph, which I still have today: plump-cheeked and startled in a too-tight sparkly top, I'm making irresolute movements with a beer glass that leave my hands a blur. When we'd finished our drinks he took me to his flat above Foschini's and fucked me against the kitchen counter, the zip of his leather jacket painfully grazing my hip. Then he dropped me back at Mr Ossendryver's before barrelling off on his motorcycle; he was going to cover a police fundraiser.

In the office, the staff photographer seemed exotic, a fish intriguingly too large for its pond, but really he fitted in perfectly, happy to play up to his role as the tame cynic, and happy to exploit its advantages, too.

I had watched his bike smoothly negotiate the twists and bends of Vermeulen Street, until finally it disappeared. He didn't look back.

When it's allowed. The phrase Mr Ossendryver used echoed in my head. I glanced at him, but he was silent now, his jaw working furiously. Was he sorry he spoke?

A Buffel slammed past, slowing to a halt and pulling up a short distance in front of us. A group of soldiers got out. The absurd thought struck me that they had heard Mr Ossendryver speak in that forbidden way about Leocardia and were here to carry him off.

With quickening strides I set off again, trying to nudge him faster up the street, slippery now from the jacaranda buds we were crushing underfoot.

'Looks like we're in for a bit of a thunderstorm!' I said.

We made it to the front door without any further complications, and his key was just sliding into the lock when, with a sinking heart, I saw him pause once more. In the sodium glare of the street lamp, Mr Ossendryver's tufty hair glowed mauve, as if coated in luminous paint. Behind him, leaves and branches trembled in a hot wind suddenly heavy with the smell of rain. I half-closed my eyes so that everything flickered just beyond my field of vision. When you open them again, I said to myself, all this weirdness will have transformed itself into some straightforward pattern that right now you're too myopic to see.

I opened my eyes and cursed my naïveté.

'It's not easy,' Mr Ossendryver said, addressing the doorknocker in low and trembling tones. 'No. And then for her own family to turn on her? But like I always say, we must pray and wait, wait and pray, and hope for better times.'

I nodded.

'Better times!' he said again. He turned his great, beaky face towards me with that odd, quick swivel that he had. 'Actually, the problem is also with the outside room,' he added. 'It's not very nice out there. These days, we use it more for a shed. She's only been back in it ...'

'... since I've been here?' I offered, and he nodded.

For a while, neither of us spoke. I imagined Mr Ossendryver with a garden rake in his hand, pushing it out of sight beneath a narrow iron bed.

'It's only temporary!' he says to the person standing motionless by the door. She's holding a toothbrush in one hand, and with the other, she's clutching a perfectly ironed pink towel.

It began to rain, softly at first, and then with greater force. Gutters gurgled, thunder rolled, monsters whistled up and down the dirty streets of Baviaan's Drift, and still Mr Ossendryver and I stood there – miserably, apologetically, pointlessly – together in the streaming dark.

I don't know why we stayed like that; it just seemed logical, all things considered. Then a tremendous thunderclap came, very near, as if in the graveyard a thousand chalky finger bones were snapping us to attention, and with the sound came Baxter, sliding a golden flank across my calf. Mr Ossendryver sighed, took out his handkerchief, gave a brief, decisive honk from his nose, and opened his front door at last.

I went to my room and threw my wet clothes on the floor. I couldn't get Mr Ossendryver's sad, kind face out of my mind. Crashing the colour bar as he was doing was no small thing, but a central transgression. In a way, I almost envied him. He had found his green light at the end of the dock.

There was an old copy of *National Geographic* lying by the bed, and to calm myself down, I started flipping through the pages. I came to a feature on birds. One picture caught my eye – I couldn't make it out. It just looked like a tangle of branches to me.

I gazed at the picture some more. And then it was as if the mass of undifferentiated leaves and twigs suddenly undulated and flashed apart, leaving a split-second space for something miraculous and new; I saw, disguised in the ripe shadows of the foliage, the shape of a marvellous creature, richly feathered and clawed, that I had not noticed before. *Scops owl*, said the caption, *a superbly camouflaged species whose dull, greyish plumage makes it almost indistinguishable when set against the branch of a tree.* The world battens down on you, the picture seemed to say, and when that happens, you resist. But what if striving to be separate from a hated system didn't require some kind of blindingly original display? What if ordinariness – rather than being the foe – was a strategy; what if it could act as a cunning concealer of strength?

I stared at the picture a while longer. It seemed to glow like the glass in a chapel window.

Then I lay down and turned out the light.

I left for Johannesburg the following week. Mr Ossendryver had arranged a lift for me with his colleague Miriam, an art teacher at the high school. She and her husband were going to spend the long Christmas break with her parents, who lived somewhere on the East Rand.

Miriam arrived promptly at half past six in the morning to pick me up. It turned out that she and her husband had just bought the car we'd be travelling in, a pale-blue Honda Ballade. Mr Ossendryver spoke out in detail and at some length in praise of the Japanese motoring industry. Then he shook my hand and told me to give my father his best wishes for a merry Christmas and a very happy new year.

I nodded; I kept on shaking his hand. I probably shook it longer and more vigorously than was strictly necessary.

'And to you, too, sir,' I said. 'A very happy new year to you, too.'

I sat down on the back seat and wound down the window a crack. When the car started moving, I pulled off my jacket and spread it across my lap. I took a pen and a notepad out of my bag and began to write to Bianca, my hand moving smoothly across the page. *The old men running the apartheid regime finally threw up their hands and declared a state of emergency in 1985 …*

By the time I remembered to turn and look out of the back window, he was gone.

The Inheritance

I woke up with a hangover, which muddled everything and meant I left the city much later than I'd planned. My grandfather would never have stood for that. His own trips to the mountains were always meticulously organised, him snapping out orders to the servants who scurried down from floor to floor and from colonnaded porch to carport, bearing the travel bags and camping gear, the braai charcoal, the flask of bitter coffee and the crates of meat and beer. From my perch beside him, I would wind down the window and stick out my head; I dug my nails into my palms and whooped as we sped faster and faster, gobbling up squatter shacks, barking dogs, prickly-pear hawkers and donkey carts and spitting them out into specks that soon vanished behind us on the plain. Today it was my turn to ease the old gullwing Mercedes into gear and make her fly. I was heading for World's View, my grandfather's weekend house, the place he'd left me in his will. It was the last place on earth I wanted to go.

World's View sits on the rim of a river gorge, at the end of a gravel road off the main highway. Eight hairpin bends wind upwards, through Camdeboo stinkwoods and mossy yellowwoods that tent the road with green. I met no traffic as I climbed, only a troop of baboons that barked defiantly down from a high rock face. I hadn't been back this way for more than twenty years, so perhaps it was no surprise that the house looked strange. Someone – Grandfather, I supposed – had clamped it round with an armoured coat: there were steel bars on every window, security gates on the doors, and on the front wall the red eye of a burglar alarm, winking from a box. Even so, the place seemed oddly vulnerable, huddled in on itself in its woodland glade: I remembered it as so much larger and more imposing than this shabby breezeblock bungalow, dwarfed by towering trees. The grass glinted; it was a frosty morning. My breath had the gloomy pallor of fog.

Yet a minute ago, easing the Mercedes down the World's View turnoff had made my tired heart soar. There across the valley were the same blue mountain tops of my childhood, and Kettle Spout Falls glinting. I could hear the same little dove crying *koer-koer, koer-koer*, and smell the same fresh, pepper scent of the soil. Like always in this high green pocket of a world, you could almost imagine that you had stumbled into an empty place, where no other human had ever been. The sense of isolation was heady. A network of roads and pathways led back to the city, but up here, out of sight, it was easy to pretend that they had all simply melted away in the mist.

'There she is! Eish, eish … welcome, welcome home!' Mrs Koen was panting down the drive; she must have been watching for the Mercedes to pass by. The Koens lived in the big green house up the hill – 'Ons Nessie', they had called it, 'Our Wee Nest'. Unlike the other half-dozen families with holiday places up here, the Koens stayed on the mountain all year round. They had become the settlement's unofficial caretakers, and the keepers of its secrets, too.

I had been part of the group, once. Long ago, when this clearing was just a campsite, before the houses came, Mrs Koen had knelt on a yellow rug cutting a birthday cake into squares and piling an extra-big, glacé-cherry-studded heap onto a paper plate just for me. I remembered the glowing tails of the mosquito coils collapsing into powder while the campfire blazed; it lit up the faces of my grandfather and Kobus Koen, locked in one of their endless games of cards. Sometimes I was woken up in the middle of the night by people laughing, shouting, or crooning volksliedjies; I lay inside my little tent, rocked by the smoke and their voices, then opened my eyes again to a daze of shifting light and the cicadas' morning song. Watching sunbirds and red-winged starlings by the stream; casting aloe branches into the bubbling water and watching them whirl away. That's it, Zoë! Good throw, my girl! Grandfather's big hands would scoop me across the boulders. Together we'd wade to the waterfall and stick our heads deep into its icy throat; his sodden black hair would flop all over his face in a funny fringe and he'd stick out his tongue to make me laugh.

Mrs Koen had changed. With her narrow face and sharp nose she still had a nervous, birdlike look but the rest of her was stout; the years of good living had left their mark. Her dark hair was faded now, the wisps scraped together in a plait that rose and fell across her chest. She nodded at me for a while in silence.

'Still so nice up here, né?' she said, and then she paused. 'You see we've been keeping it safe for you all this time!'

I didn't know what to say to that, so I kept quiet. Mrs Koen shook and quivered and wrung her white hands some more. She said that I should come by and say hello to Kobus, to just drop by for a coffee or a drink or a meal, whenever I wanted, or perhaps I would like to borrow a DVD; it was no bother, the two of them would be at home all weekend. All this time she turned a house key over and over in her palm. The greying stranger in the crumpled clothes who stood before her was like a foreigner, I could see that. I relished her discomfort, it gave me a bit of strength.

She unlocked World's View; same top notes of varnish and Sunlight Soap, same undertones of drains and damp. A fire had been laid in the grate, and a basket filled with kindling. A bed had been made up with a pink quilted satin coverlet and the little fridge was stuffed with goodies, including a bottle of expensive Boland champagne; Mrs Koen had gone to some trouble. On the table was a plastic bag filled with prickly pears, a hurried afterthought. Those would have come from one of the farm stalls down on the plain.

I caught a glimpse of my face in the mirror above the fireplace; I looked washed-out, pale as a sheet of paper. Mrs Koen's scrutiny was confronting me with a hopelessly outdated version of myself. Where had she gone, the wide-eyed student who signed manifestos, marched for Mandela's release and wore an attitude of perpetual outrage at the world's injustices? Vanished, subsumed into a fifteen-month marriage, divorce, a series of part-time jobs teaching art to kids in schools, and more recently, a kind of drift. They'd let me go at the Sacred Heart Primary four months back; the downturn was taking its toll. I'd been relying on bits and pieces of private tuition to keep me going, but I was barely paying the bills.

Just drop by any time, Mrs Koen said again. I knew she was trying to be friendly, but every word she spoke made me feel more mutinous and less inclined to speak. She asked me how the road was round Celesteville. Kobus had heard on the wireless that a big veld fire was burning near there, up in the hills, and now it was threatening to sweep right down to the highway. The winds all that week had been strong.

I made an effort. I hadn't seen it, I said, but I'd got stuck behind two big water trucks that must have been heading up that way and thanks to them I'd crawled at a snail's pace for miles. It made me laugh, I said to her, thinking of what my grandfather would have done in my place. You know how he hated that kind of thing, how it drove him mad not being in control of every single situation! And Mrs Koen's face lit up, as if my mentioning his name was the spark she had been waiting for all along.

When at last she left, I took a walk down to the bathing pool, using the steeper path where the trees make a canopy over a dry streambed. I moved in a greenish tunnel of leaves and stones, the frost in the air just spiking. I passed the big granite outcrop where the path narrows, and arum lilies whiten the ground between the ferns and fallen branches. From the biggest boulder in the middle of the bathing pool I could see three holiday houses strung out along the top of the ridge, one of them double-storeyed and quite grand.

I sat on the cold stone and looked at the forest: at the dust cross-hatching the sun and shade and the dry leaves dropping down. At first glance it looked peaceful enough, but after a while the space began to flicker slightly at the edges, and a kind of fearfulness gripped my mind. In the shadowy hush of the water and the trees I felt my grandfather's presence. Two weeks dead, it was as if he had returned from some other place to penetrate the midday haze, tinged as it was with the grey chill of winter; moving slowly but insistently, a long breath enveloping my rock, whitening the air, feeling its way up. I leaped to my feet, and shook myself. I couldn't allow myself to let him touch me. Not now. Not just yet.

Mrs Koen had left her number by the telephone. Tossing the scrap of paper to the floor, I sat down on the sofa with the bag of prickly pears. Cut the ends off first, using a fork as a spear – that's how you do it, Zoë, my girl. Make a big slit down each pear's spiny belly, grasp the cut and tear it open, then the fruit comes free – see?

As I ate the ruby pears, spitting out the seeds, I marshalled the facts again, like a mantra. A successful lawyer in the city, my grandfather had named me as his heir when my father died. He installed my mother and me in a flat above the Caltex garage on the old Port Elizabeth Road, made a point of having me round frequently to the big house in Market Square, and took me camping every summer with the Koens. I adored him, lolling in his reflected light. We were co-conspirators from the start: I was the only one privy to his secret life of Saturday mornings, stepping inside the big white Mercedes that shrugged off the Caltex garage forecourt, and then our road, in great bounds of speed. The barber's, the betting shop, the Neptune

Café: wherever he went, I was welcome, with my own high stool by the cash register as he chaffed the Neptune waitress with the frizzy yellow curls.

The part I didn't care for was when he'd leave me waiting outside the bar of the Rhodes Hotel. No need to mention it to your ma, hey, my girl? And he would wink as he parked the car and vanished indoors. Occasionally Mimi, the hotelier's little white lapdog, would come out to greet me, flicking her petunia tail in my direction before slumping down in the doorway with trembling tongue. But usually, my only diversion was the street – the donkey-cart drivers shouting at their animals; the long queues endlessly forming for buses to the township at Makana's Kop; the hawker women who ruled the pavements, some old and skinny with crushed, careworn faces, others young and ample with hard, ferocious stares.

It usually took about an hour in the humid drowsiness of my grandfather's car for the lines between reality and fantasy to start to blur. The flame trees blooming all along the street would start to multiply into one bright mass; although the usual throng pressed past, their movements became slow and fuzzy, like an old film. Time ground down, the shopkeepers standing frozen in their doorways, waiting. Everything was suspended, sometimes for aeons, until suddenly my grandfather was there on the steps again, tossing away a match, drawing hard on his cigarette, surveying the town. Standing beneath the glittering panes of the hotel fanlight, Mimi lolling at his feet, my grandfather had the power to speed up the day, restoring it, whole, to its normal pace. Yet I never quite let myself believe he remembered my existence until I'd seen him turn and smile, and salute my frantic wave.

Some time around my eighth birthday he visited Wepener, the Free State town named for his ancestor, and brought back photographs of a bronze bust that glowered from a plinth in the old town hall. Grandfather said: 'See how the Kommandant has my profile, Zoë?

And maybe yours too, once you're grown.' I stared at the bust with its pinched mouth and ugly, jutting brow. The stories that went with it were nasty at first, and then merely dull, but he invested so much in them. Once, when I made the mistake of looking bored, my grandfather went very red in the face and stopped talking; his eyes gleamed, fierce and faraway at the same time, and I realised with astonishment that I had hurt him. He was so preoccupied with his claims to a glorious Afrikaner past, and I was, of course, his work in progress, his best and only hope for an heir.

While the Boer troops hid in their tents, my grandfather told me, wringing their hands and wrangling over how best to oust the Sotho king from his mountaintop kraal, our ancestor seized the chance to show his mettle. With only 400 loyal volunteers he stormed the citadel, flying towards the summit. With no thought for himself he urged his men forward, sparking courage in the hearts of each. Our side was vastly outnumbered, my grandfather kept repeating, with enemy soldiers clustering thickly around the Royal Palace like flies round a hunk of meat. Yet it took until sunset for the last of those good men to fall. Our ancestor died a hero's death right beneath the summit of the mountain, there at Rafutho Pass. Ja-nee, in the manner of his passing he had nothing to berate himself for, my grandfather remarked in a tired voice, smoothing a hand over the soft, pink patch on the top of his head. That is why the Basotho warriors cooked and ate his heart that night, believing that in this manner they might acquire some of his bravery. And my grandfather mounted an enormous print of the Kommandant's bust in a heavy frame and hung it in his dining room, where it stared grimly down at us as the maid served the Sunday roast.

I was twelve when I finally told him I wouldn't go camping in the mountains any more. As summer approached, I prepared a host of reasons: first, I needed to be busy with my schoolwork, but also, gloriously, I had been invited to stay at the seaside with Dawn de

Wet, a mark of approval I was desperate not to ignore. Dawn was captain of the netball team, with silvery blonde hair so fine it took your breath away. Summoned to the telephone to explain myself, I mumbled in the way that my grandfather couldn't stand.

'You want to go where with the netball team?' he cried. 'Speak up, my child! I cannot understand a single word that you say.' With the toe of my sandal, I scraped at the mosquito bite behind my left knee. It was a muggy evening in early summer. 'Are you still there?' my grandfather bellowed. Then he slammed down the phone. Twenty minutes later, I heard the unmistakable roar of the Mercedes outside. The sound sank to a rich grumble, then stopped. There was a silence. I gaped at my mother, then bolted up the stairs to bed.

My grandfather's opening volley was aimed at his daughter-in-law; something about wanting a brandy. I heard the fridge door slam; she would have been fetching the ice.

'Ja, the bloody mamparas forgot to put on a cover, you know?' I heard my grandfather say. 'What can a man do, eh.' The new driveway his workmen had laid only the day before had been ruined by some small night animal stealing across the wet concrete, seeking the freedom of the veld.

My mother's reply, when it came, was indistinct, but went on for some time. She was a woman used to waiting for her turn to speak, yet she would talk right over you if there was something she really wanted to say. It took a lot of people from my grandfather's generation unawares. Silence from downstairs. Then I heard the squeaky, scraping sound of a kitchen chair being abruptly shifted, and his brisk tread upon the steps. A wire of light from the corridor sprang beneath my door. Squeezing my eyes tight shut, I turned my face to the wall.

What could I say to my granddad? He never explained anything directly to me, anyway. Maybe he thought that he and I would always feel the same about things just because we were related; the same tunes marched in our blood. But I had treachery in me, blue like a stain. There was a side of him that I always tried to ignore, and it came out the strongest on those trips to the mountains, when he sat around the campfire with his friends. All that thundering on about political doom and disaster. All one big slide down into a future they feared. To me, at twelve, the spectacle of all those shouting grown-ups with their long red, shiny faces had long stopped being scary. No, the main problem was just that they were so very dull. It was like their gatherings were scripted, you always knew exactly what everyone was going to say.

I did not know what to do. I didn't want to hurt him – despite everything I still belonged to him, my sensibilities untried. But suddenly it came to me, how to shock him into his own peculiar brand of shyness, a state of vulnerability so fierce it was almost hostile. My monthlies had recently begun for the first time, I told him, still with my face to the wall. It was a curse we women bore, of course, I went on, warming to my theme, and of course I was trying my hardest to bear it. Dawn de Wet – she, for one, couldn't stand the type of girl who whimpered about such things; I had often heard her say it. But the bleeding – well, it was fierce; yes, really bad, and came in floods, suddenly, with awful pains that shot through you like fiery arrows. That was why, for the meantime, I thought it best not to leave my bed.

My grandfather sighed, but did not speak. He just sat there; I knew he'd be stroking his moustache. Then he patted my feet beneath the coverlet, and I felt his weight lift away from the bed. He was gone, and then I longed to be with him, of course, and felt the lack of him keenly through all the summer days that followed.

All this happened in the eighties, at the end of Afrikaner rule. The years after Mandela came to power were violent and volatile; my grandfather must have felt – what? Fury? Shame? Defeat? He took to writing letters to the papers, bitter screeds about falling standards, in his fine old-fashioned Free State Afrikaans. He'd read them aloud to my mother and me when we came round for Sunday lunch, but I don't think he ever posted a single one. The wastepaper baskets in that house were always full of crumpled fists of discarded paper, uncurling slowly in the dark.

Building World's View was a more measured response to the crisis. Steeped in the old apartheid solitudes, maybe he thought withdrawing to the mountain tops would somehow keep a real separation between his old way of life and the new. That crowd down there? Slit your throat as soon as look at you, you'll see.

The house-warming party was held on a sparkling summer's day. I was at college in Cape Town by then, smoking marijuana, striking poses in my home-made African print mini-dresses and pretending to study art. World's View was full of people, all the familiar faces – all the old group from the campsite. My mother and the servants went in and out from the kitchen with platters of meat and bottles of beer. My grandfather sat in a chair on the back stoep, chuckling indulgently, his white shirt open to his grey wolf's chest.

'But you lied to me!' I yelled at him in my head. I imagined that I was standing on the top steps leading down to the stoep, that I saw him slowly turn and smile, and salute my presence with a wave. All the other people in the room were staring, their conversations suspended, waiting to hear me speak. 'You *greedy* – you stupid old fool, you built this house illegally, without a permit, and it's all a mess and you've no right to be here on this land at all!'

In my mind's eye, my grandfather pretended to look mystified. 'But why not, my dear? No one's using the site. No one's losing out. And really, if the new government isn't up to the job of legally protecting its property, why is that my fault?'

I'd shouted much the same things at Mr Koen's nephew, Simon, the suave young attorney who was handling my grandfather's estate. I'd asked to see the deeds to the house and he'd handed me a boxful of hunting permits, signed by the chief of a local tribe.

Simon had spread out his plump hands with their impeccably manicured fingertips. 'The old man was a law unto himself. We both know that.'

'So after he went sneaking up the mountainside, your aunt and uncle followed! And the de Jagers, the Koekemoers and all the rest! And everyone just keeps *schtum*!' I was so aghast, I could hardly get the words out. 'That chief from back then. He'll have grown-up sons and daughters by now – they could be lawyers themselves. Do you really expect to get away with it?'

I'd heard about this scam before. There'd been a similar case down on the Transkei coast, years before; it had been splashed across all the papers. You and your friends stumbled across a remote patch of vacant state land – perhaps land held in trust for local tribes. You found a headman to act as a go-between with the relevant chief. At your first meeting, you pressed into the chief's hand some cash and a bottle of brandy, or whatever constituted his drink of choice. The chief arranged for you to attend a meeting of the tribal authority, where your request for a plot was unanimously approved. Your roof beams rose high, and every year you paid that chief a handful of coins for a hunting permit, or a fishing permit, or whatever it was that the old man was actually empowered to sign. Then, surrendering the city spaces to their fate, you withdrew to your holiday house and fortified it, and took a furtive pleasure in your view.

'At least take a trip up there, see it again before you rush into any decisions,' Koen Junior had soothed. 'You've lived away in Joburg all this time, but your grandfather never stopped hoping you'd come back home to the Eastern Cape to live. He spoke of you so often.'

But while my visit to World's View was having an effect, it wasn't the one the Koens wanted. What my grandfather had done had retrospective power and now in some strange way it was reshuffling our relationship. A kind of coldness was spreading through it. I had always thought of him as the heart of the family, as well as the head, but his calculation in giving me the house was plain. The land and I were both there for the taking – that's what he thought. He simply altered the facts to suit his inner eye. To him, I would always be the devoted granddaughter, not the stranger who only called at Christmas time, who had frittered away twenty years in a faraway town, moving restlessly from job to job, and from man to man, shifting her possessions around shabby flats in suburban streets I didn't care if I never saw again. Naturally, my grandfather thought, his granddaughter would rush to lay claim to his beloved view. Naturally I would step into his shoes, continue his deception, and cover up his crime.

Something clattered in my dreams and I woke with a jump. I'd fallen asleep on the sofa. Mrs Koen was knocking on the door again, and it was already late afternoon. I let her in and listened as she started to talk about ordinary things, wireless reports, and extra blankets, and whether I had had some lunch. I just stared at her. I felt tired and hung-over and sick at heart. I would have to call the police when I got back to the city. There would be rows and recriminations, and it would go on and on, with eviction orders and court cases and all the houses needing to be demolished. But I couldn't say anything to her just yet. I needed to get away – from the muddle of it, and Mrs Koen's frail grey plait, and the cold light coming up from the valley that was glittering in the mirror. Mumbling my goodbyes, I picked up my keys and fled.

As I pulled away, I caught a glimpse of the valley and the mountains, their great slopes thick with cloud. Would I ever be free of the place? No, because the past was not done with here, I thought to myself; its problems drip-fed into the present, muddying it endlessly. In forgotten places like this one you saw it most clearly, the old ways unextinguished and forever edging forward, smudging boundaries, making a fool of the new maps, nicking at your heels. And then a small voice came unbidden: *you could start a new life up here,* it said. *You could live rent-free.* The voice spoke with calculated calm. *You need somewhere to catch your breath for a while, to think straight. Perhaps you could start to paint again. Why not keep the secret? Why not say you never knew?*

Outside Celesteville, the hillsides were black and smouldering, although most of the blaze had died down. You could see that the veld fire had burned on both sides of the road, reaching from the mountain slopes right down to the railway line. All that was left were tiny nests of sparks and a few livid, quivering rills of fire that crackled down to the verges and hissed. There was still quite a lot of smoke. On the horizon, the highway snaked into another line of hills, thrusting further and further into the wilderness. It was beginning to get dark. I drove on to the lawyers' offices, faster and faster, my hands shaking, sparks plucking at my heels.

The New Equality

The hotel had been hit by the blackout, but it didn't matter because the place looked even more perfect in the dark. From all around the shadowy lobby came little barks and whoops of words and laughter, and sudden intimate wafts of breath and sweating flesh, as if the people inside had become one giant creature. The dim staircase, the deep alcoves above Camilla's head, bloomed with a secret promise of warm rooms that waited at the end of long corridors where the half-light could thicken to black. Something brushed the back of her head, deliciously – a lynx-tail? a lyre-bird feather? – and by the time the concierge arrived with candles, their long shadows crazily striping the walls, she felt such a devouring charge of anticipation that her hands trembled; she had to hold on to the edge of the reception desk to make herself dignified again.

Power cuts were driving everybody in Johannesburg mad that summer. Every person you met had a horror story – the aromatherapist shot by robbers as she screamed for help, her remote-controlled gates stuck shut; the hedge-fund manager who died mid-op from a stroke when the hospital's back-up generator failed. But here, the hotel staff were all smiles as they busied themselves in the mid-afternoon gloom, toting torches, a pillow, even a dish of jittery jellies from some blacked-out fridge. Like dear little stage-hands, Camilla thought with satisfaction, all scuttling tirelessly between their tasks, setting the scene for what she very much hoped was going to be the fuck of a goddamn lifetime.

'Lumka, bhuti, move, man!' Extraordinary, the type of people you saw in these places. A meat-mountain of a woman was emerging from the ladies', a real character, tilting slowly on swollen legs. Her path had been blocked by the cleaner, a fragile youth nudging a rag along the quarry tiles with a broom the size of a roadsweeper. 'You trying to cosy up to me in the dark, hey?' Her sweating face was topped by a roll of peroxided hair, a husk of maize against the brown earth of her skin. The young man at Camilla's side gave a snort of laughter and squeezed her hand.

He gets it too, Camilla thought, exultantly; talk about hitting gold. A five-star playground gone feral in the blackout; it was sexy as hell. Reverting to third world type, you might say, but with all the right luxury add-ons, from goose down pillowcases to lavender-scented sheets.

But then – was this really happening? – the receptionist looked up from her phone call and explained, quite politely, with none of the usual apathy or barely concealed ill will, that Camilla and the young man could not check in. The blackout was forcing the hotel to close, the back-up system was playing up; standards could not be guaranteed. Head office orders. Madam would perhaps like to take a brochure? And now some busybody was propping open the electric front doors so they could leave, letting in a gritty breeze along with the blinding afternoon light.

In the harsh sun of the hotel car park the young man pressed Camilla back against her BMW and slid a hand between her legs. She waited, not quite melting into the embrace, before shrugging him away with a martyred sigh.

'Well, no good hanging about here much longer,' she said.

Beyond his shoulder, across a wasteland of litter and crushed glass, it was just possible to make out the Magaliesberg mountains. Down below flowed the grimy city, glittering in the heat. All exactly as the two of them had left it twenty minutes ago, and yet sunk in an air of listlessness now, as if attuned to their bad luck.

But the young man pulled her back. 'We need to find another place. We're running out of time, Mrs P. C'mon, let's go!' he said, nuzzling in her neck like a dog.

Again, she twirled away. 'I don't know what the point of that would be. The blackout's city-wide, nothing else will be open, you heard what the receptionist said.'

The truth was, she felt guilty. The afternoon had started out so well, the two of them leaving the restaurant after the second bottle of wine, soused in lust, looking for a place to suit their purpose. Yet she – playing the madcap – had stupidly turned down the first two hotels they'd come across, insisting on holding out for something with a bit more *flair*.

The young man narrowed his eyes now and took off his cap, showing a brown, close-shaven scalp covered with tiny whorls of stubborn black hair.

'Camilla. I have to work tonight and you said Lola and Tom would only be at your sister's till six. We've got no time, so let's go … heartless as always, hey? You don't understand how much I need you, my baby.'

How adorable he was. She was always absurdly pleased when he remembered the names of her children. Yet she spoke of them seldom, not wishing to remind him that she was twenty years older than he.

Heads bowed, she and the young man sank back into the BMW's refrigerated embrace. Driving south on the highway, the air was full of dust; the exhausts of passing trucks and minibus taxis made it dustier. Soon they were marooned in the inside slow lane, crawling behind a long queue of cars.

The blackout had killed the lights at Jan Smuts Avenue and Jellicoe and streams of impatient motorists, horns blaring, were taking directions from a traffic policewoman, her hands stuttering nervously in a pair of grubby white gloves.

'Mrs P ... tell me all over again what underwear you've got on.'

He was smiling at her, looking her up and down. Yes, look at me, she thought, arching her spine at him defiantly. That morning, as she did every day, she'd taken pains to tweeze away the grey hairs on her head, to spray herself with the perfume bought on last year's Paris trip, to select the highest pair of Ferragamo heels. For she was still not old.

'Oh, Bheki. You know all that's no good – right now.'

'No. What a mess, hey? What a mess this city is.'

A red van was rolling by. 'That's one of Michael Bernstein's trucks,' the young man said, suddenly. 'The sound man we used on the Superbowl shoot? Oh, God! Camilla –'

The young man was an intern at the broadcasting company where her husband was the CEO.

'It isn't him driving. Just some guy who works for him, Bheki. He can't hurt us.'

She leaned across to the young man and kissed him. She fancied she could still smell on his skin the intoxicating scent of the burning candle-wax.

His boy's face – so vivid, so excitable – jumped at the feel of her mouth. 'God, you're so good,' he said. 'Ah, Camilla. You know I can't stop thinking about you. I want to hear your voice even if I've got no reason to call and feel like kicking myself afterwards for coming across like an idiot. And it's going to get worse, I think, before it gets better.'

'Relax, silly. You mustn't stress yourself out so ...'

And she watched while he lay still in the passenger seat with his eyes shut. Under her hand his slender, cotton-covered shoulders were warm to the touch. His jeans had been neatly pressed. Somebody must be doing his ironing for him, as she still occasionally did her husband's, and the idea that it was a woman – a woman unknown to her – pricked at her unpleasantly and wouldn't settle down. She stared sideways at his narrow face.

'It was also fine, you know,' the young man said suddenly, 'just knowing you. Just hanging out together with a cup of coffee. Playing pool in that bar after the Christmas party with you and Trevor and Sipho. I used to tell them that I had a crush on you.'

Oh, lord, not now, she thought. It was one of his lapses of confidence.

'So … you wish we'd never got this thing started, hmm?' Gently, she lifted his hand and began giving each of his fingertips a kiss. But the young man refused to soften.

'That's not it at all.' His hand twitched away from her, coming to light first on his chest, then his lap, in that restless way he had. 'I wanted you from the beginning. You know that very well,' he said. 'But it's more difficult now. You know I never … this isn't how I imagined it would be. This business of not having our own place to go. And the creeping about. I didn't put myself so low when we began, or you either.'

They were inching their way north along Oxford Road, some sort of additional hold-up having been caused by a turning truck, belching soot.

'I kind of thought you'd let me sleep with you a few times and then you'd get bored and things would go on as before,' the young man went on. 'We were such good friends in the beginning, don't you remember? Friends forever, you said. And that's all different now. Because we have to pretend. You know, Trevor asked me straight out the other day and of course I lied like a pro. But I never used to think of myself as secretive.'

Soothe him. 'Look,' Camilla began. 'I know it's a very unstable situation. But bored with you? My darling, I've told you so many times

I was desperate before you came, I was slowly going numb from the inside out … I was almost dead. Now we have this thing together, and don't you see that that's the fuel of it – this amazing chance to just *bathe* in each other – it's simply impossible to lay down a strict way forward. We need to stay in the moment and just go with it without questionings. Without question, I mean …'

Get a grip, girl. She rolled her window down, letting in a pounce of air that smelled of sewage. Behind them reared the grey spike of the Hillbrow Tower; in front lay the suburbs of the north, her home. That was where the swimming pools were, the jacaranda-lined boulevards, the chrome-and-glass shopping malls, the dogs and razor wire. The young man had grown up in the south-west, in an area populous and cramped, and until recently, more or less invisible. Apartheid map makers used simply to ignore Tembisa, Mamelodi, Soshanguve, Carletonville: that welter of broken-down suburbs bred by the dark. But see, here was progress, the new equality writ large: the whole city was united now, every teeming street gone dim. Stolen power pumping into her and Bheki instead, her hands twitching on the steering wheel, betraying her to the world with every flick-switch surge.

The wine had left her with a terrible thirst. She could have done with some water to drink.

'Listen to me! You bloody deaf, man?' The guy in the Subaru alongside her was cursing the hawkers cruising between the jammed cars, proffering CDs, trays of oranges, hands-free kits for mobile phones. A blue bucket, swept up high in a boy's hands, came bobbing towards her. No, thank you, she signalled to the boy. No windscreen wash today.

'But I feel like it's marking me, somehow. I mean, what is it you see when you look at my face?' Bheki was asking, with emphasis.

The window washer boy returned to the Subaru. Dropping the bucket onto the bonnet of the car, he flashed the driver a grin and began smearing the dust on the windscreen with a filthy cloth. 'Hey, you! I said no!' the man shouted. Voice rising. Snarling with rage and resentment. 'You hear me?' His voice was screechy. 'Get away from my car, man!'

For a moment the boy stood indecisively by the Subaru's window. He picked up the bucket again. His hair was woven into thin black braids and he ran a hand through these and muttered something, something angry and equally insulting, as the man yelled at him. 'Listen to me!'

A thick-legged girl in an Orlando Pirates T-shirt had materialised beside the boy, a squeegee in one hand and a wiper blade in the other. Motioning him away.

He didn't move. Stood shifting from foot to sneakered foot.

'Fuck off, kaffir!' the man yelled again. Reaching out of the car and grabbing the handle of the bucket just as the boy lifted his other arm, took aim and fired.

Jesus. Heart thudding, scared sick, moaning, Camilla shut her eyes and hunched her forearms over her head, jerking onto her side as she had heard you should do in these situations, because then they would get you in the ribcage where there was more bone to protect your guts.

But the gunshot didn't come. When she opened her eyes, the Subaru driver was staring straight ahead, his red face still foxy with rage. The boy with the bucket had strolled away, moving on to a different car further down the line. As he went, he turned and made a gun of his forefinger, cocking it again at the Subaru. *Bam.*

Her pulse still raced as she fumbled for the BMW's window controls; drop your shoulders, she told herself; relax. No one got mugged, today.

She risked a glance at Bheki. Their eyes met, but only for a second, because the expression on his face was embarrassed and strained. Outside, the CD hawkers were sauntering past, snickering. *Check the umlungus losing it, big-style.*

Camilla bit her lip. She wasn't a racist, naturally; she and Jeremy had tons of black friends. But she did have certain instincts – well, it was all common sense, really – that in her short time with Bheki she had somehow not found the right moment to explain. Wasn't she a silly old goose? But terror for her wore a black face; yes, she felt that.

'Bheki?' She cleared her throat. But his gaze had flickered; with relief, she watched his attention race away to something new. He was reaching out to trace the outline of her breast. Her nipple hardened obediently, and the young man smiled.

'Camilla. I don't know ...' His caress grew harder, he licked his lips as he spoke. 'Let's just take this thing for all that it's worth, man. Ah, but where can we go? Where can we go, like *now* ...'

Camilla said, weakly: 'Goodness, I hope you don't mean to take advantage of me, Mr Mzi?'

Her head pounded, Bheki groaned, the traffic moved at last. She had a sense that they were avoiding something, but felt far too stressed to work out what it was.

By the time they were clear of Sandton Central, the late afternoon light had taken on the lurid, electric sheen that meant a thunderstorm was hatching. Outside a candlelit coffee shop on a quiet parade, customers sat chatting beneath a tall jacaranda. A young woman leaned over a buggy, coaxing her crying infant's attention towards something high up.

Camilla parked right outside, where she and Bheki could easily be seen. After all, today they were innocent. She was a married woman, hands full with the work of raising two healthy, well-adjusted children, stepping out for a quick cup of tea with a friend.

A poster advertising a brand of Caribbean rum dominated a nearby wall. A blue sheet of water, spitting foam, arched above a paddling surfer, ready to shred the doll-like body in a roil of sand

and rock. Camilla saw herself walking barefoot over sandy grass on her grandmother's beachfront plot thirty years ago, near a water tank beside a frangipani tree. That day, with its hot sun and the sweet smell of the rainwater that spurted when the tank's beaky tap was turned, always came back when she thought of being a child. She thought: *I wish we could run away. I wish I could take him on a trip back to the Eastern Cape, just the two of us, get away from it all ...*

Her headache had not gone, but the snarled-up knot of nervous energy inside her had slackened to admit something she had not allowed herself to feel for weeks – a kind of exhaustion.

She turned to the young man slumped at her side.

'Just a quick pit stop, hey?' He didn't stir. In her tiredness, she found herself resorting to the cajoling, sing-song voice she sometimes used with her children: 'Now, what in the world could that woman be staring at up in the tree?'

Bheki shaded his eyes with his hand. 'A kid's balloon, I think.' He jumped out of the car and picked up a stone.

The toy – a metallic silver bubble, with a ribbon for a string – was trapped between two jacaranda branches. With a smooth, almost lazy gesture, Bheki raised the stone to his shoulder, fixing the balloon in his sights. The impact of the blow knocked it sideways, where it shivered, but stayed put. Its ribbon drooped crookedly down. White satin, slightly soiled.

'Bheki! I'm thirsty, my darling. Bheki, leave that. Let's go inside.'

But Bheki's jaw was set, his brow furrowed. He was intent on his new task. He stooped down for another stone, and another as the balloon-string twirled out of reach.

'Tricky little number,' he said, almost to himself, with a soft, excited laugh.

He would have liked to crush it in his frustration, she sensed – the soft roundness, the wet shine of the globe's slippery surface was intoxicating to him as it trembled up above. His eyes shone as he turned to look for new pebbles, as he jumped to get a better aim. Yet the thing refused to budge.

Camilla fell silent, watching him. She saw the probing fingers weighing each stone in turn, the precision of the brown arms that rose and fell, Bheki's cool-eyed, restless gaze. She had gone after him seeking a plaything, a pet, but he was infinitely more powerful than that. She saw for the first time his hold on her, the reach of him into her most private imaginings. She saw the emptiness – desolate and cold – that would rise to claim her should her hold on him flicker and fail.

A weight of dread seemed to paralyse her. After a while, she said: 'We'd better get a move on, you know. We're miles from the office yet. Your shift –'

'And now for the bullseye!' he said, taking careful aim at the tree.

He had unearthed a rock so large he had to pick it up with both hands.

Dumbly, she sat in the car and looked at him. She moistened her lips. She could feel the movement of her heart.

Dry Run

It was a disaster, the opposite of how you want your first time to be. Thandiwe's cousin in Port Alfred had jumped off a bridge for a dare, never dreaming of the consequences. So she'd done this … you know, *damage* to herself, Thandiwe told Joanne, but in the most public way. Trickles of blood had clouded the waters of the Kowie River and the back of her white swimsuit as she splashed, sobbing, to the shore. The other school kids who'd seen her spread the story around and that's when the bullying began. Thandiwe's cousin had endured months of taunts about being los and gagging for it, and now she'd been put on an antidepressant pill.

'Listen, man, I feel so bad for her. Really, I do,' Thandiwe said. Her plump mouth opened wide to admit a glistening forkful of the roasted sheep's head she was scooping from a newsprint wrap. The animal's lips were shrivelled and scorched right down to the grey jawbone, yet it looked like they were smiling – trapped, it seemed to Joanne, in the echo of some derisive joke.

'And she's only fourteen, same as us. But I scheme she'll never get a boyfriend now. Okes round here? How's she going to find someone who'll handle her popping her cherry in such a messed up way, in front of the whole damn world?'

Thandiwe had been talking for ages, all the time it had taken the girls to walk from the school gates in Rhodes Place down the hill past the bus station. You could hear the buses long before you saw them, snorting and roaring, bored simply unto madness by the sheer tedium of it all, Joanne thought, by the same flies every day and the same dust, the same smell of offal and roasting mielie-cobs rising from smoky braziers, and the press of township commuters impatient to be home. It was a hot afternoon in November, with only a few weeks to go before the long summer break.

'Maybe it shouldn't be anyone's business, and anyway, who cares about a few dumb bitch gossips, hey?' Thandiwe was stabbing at the sheep's lolling purple tongue with her plastic fork. 'But now the whole thing has given my dad these … *thoughts* about me. Boys and me. The proper way to behave – all that. He's so uptight. If he had his way, I wouldn't go out with a guy for, like, fifty years. Know what I mean?'

Etienne was also a stickler for proper behaviour. In the beginning, Joanne had not found this strange: after all, he was forty-five, indisputably a grown-up. Although that description wasn't really quite right. Maybe a month ago she would still have thought of him that way, but now, caught off-balance as she was by the thing that snaked between them, the term no longer seemed to fit.

'Twenty minutes,' he had said yesterday, looking sideways at her as he scooped up his shoulder-holster from the car's footwell. 'We said we'd meet here at eighteen hundred hours. We agreed on a time, but now here you come twenty minutes late. You looking to pick a fight with me, Joanne?'

When Joanne – aghast, tearful, and, she knew, unflatteringly brick-red from running all the way to their secret place behind the Botanical Gardens – had stammered out how Miss Dougmore had kept the whole form back and for absolutely no reason, he took his pistol out of its holster and gave her nose the tiniest push.

'Keep your tits on,' he had said.

Etienne had a gun because he was a police sergeant, with specialist training in stock theft and farm offences. His silver car was part of the package, although his bakkie was his real pride and joy. He had told her these things the day they first met, the radiant and stupendously amazing day they had talked for nearly an hour, when, instead of dropping her at home, he had taken a side road up to a viewpoint he knew on Mountain Drive. Afterwards, when he finally said goodbye and she stood at her gate and watched his car streak away, Joanne had heard the sound of gunfire blaring from the house across the road. The old couple that lived there always had their TV turned up too loud. Fighting crime in that dark world of danger was Etienne's life, she thought – it was no surprise he had leapt to fight off her tormenter during her hour of need. It wasn't her fault he had unexpectedly veered off down that little side road; it wasn't her fault he kept asking if she knew she looked like a young Shania Twain.

Just a few weeks ago she had still been the old Joanne – the one who dawdled home past the bus station after school, exam revision work making a dreary boulder of her bag. Just a few weeks ago, she had gone to flick through the gossip magazines at the Central News Agency, looking for titbits about the London model whose passion for a drug-addicted rock star was hurtling her towards career suicide. Later, she stopped in front of Lily's Larger Ladies' Fashions, where a headless dummy sported a party dress that looked like a rotting peach. A place like London was so huge you probably never even saw a horizon. Here, even in the high street, you could see bushveld clutching at the valley rim, beyond the Methodist church and the Record Ranch and the two banks and the estate agent's office and the beaten-down donkey-carts that went clip-clopping by. 'Three more years and the world's your oyster,' her father had said. 'You got the brains for it, my girl, so pass those exams and you can take your pick of any university you want.' Three more years of suffocation in back-of-beyond hell, then she and her stupid life might finally go somewhere. Or, even, begin.

That day, still dreaming of London, she'd stopped short in the middle of the road. Out of nowhere a skinny kid on a bicycle had sliced past, swerving to avoid her and then powering away, yelling hideous words as he went. She'd been shocked almost to tears, like a little kid. Exam papers, books, a half-open pencil case – they all slithered traitorously from her schoolbag as she lunged for the kerb.

In front of her, a man was loading a crate of beer into the boot of a silver car. He was about Joanne's height, but powerfully built, green-eyed like a cat, olive-skinned, with slightly curling black hair. He closed the boot and smiled at her. He wore a grey suit with a waistcoat, cut in an Edwardian style. His manners were old-fashioned, too. 'You OK, Miss?' he'd said, very gently and softly. 'You look like you got a fright. You need a hand?'

Just then the boy on the bike swooped back, spoiling for a second round. 'Watch where you're walking next time, kak-for-brains!' he was shouting.

Astonishingly, the beautiful man sprang out into the road and grabbed the boy around the neck. 'That's enough!' he barked. 'Get out of here before I shove your head up your arse and carry you around like a suitcase!' And he tossed the boy and his bike aside with a clatter.

Joanne was speechless. She felt she didn't know what to do or where to look. She stared dumbly at the beautiful man's waistcoat buttons, pearly as milk teeth.

'Thank you,' she whispered.

The man smiled at her again, opening his wallet and taking out a badge. 'I'm a police officer,' he had said. 'That's why I'm allowed to tell moegoes like that where to go. Can I offer you a lift?'

Joanne shook her head. But something in her flickered and sparked. Then it spoke to her, privately. 'Poor baby!' it jeered. 'Too shy? Too frightened to cope?'

If she turned her head just slightly, Joanne could see her reflection in the window of the man's car. She knew she didn't look like a baby. She was tall for her age, with the makings of a summer tan from lying for hours in the garden last weekend. The wind was tugging her hair from its fastenings and fanning it about her face. The tears in her eyes would probably be making them sparkle. Her cheeks felt hot.

She wondered if the man was still looking at her, seeing what she was seeing.

The boy picked up his bicycle and began pedalling unsteadily away. 'Bitch!' he called, not so loudly this time, as he wobbled back around the corner.

Joanne stooped to gather her spilled pencils, but the man was quicker than she was. 'Your surname,' he said, straightening up and turning her denim pencil case around with probing fingertips. He was studying the letters she'd stencilled on last year, in that dumb curly script. 'It sounds Afrikaans, like my name – Etienne. Wouldn't it be something if you and I were related?'

And at that, the secret thing within her seemed to smile, to swell vastly. How about that, then? she told it.

Never taking his eyes from her face, Etienne said, still softly but quite firmly, 'Shall we go?'

Stepping into the car, a shiver ran through her body, like she was tumbling into deep water.

Right from the start, it was a struggle not to tell. Right from the start, Joanne longed, at the very least, to wallpaper her cellphone with Etienne's picture, but she didn't dare. After the way he'd gone on and on about the reasons to keep their thing a secret, she felt much too frightened, yet part of her was desperate to tell Thandiwe, if only to brag. She imagined how she would break the news, how Thandiwe would stop in her tracks and stare at her, eyes widening in envy and surprise.

'Jirre, get away, man, you're joking me! Are you serious right now?'

'It's true, Thandiwe. So in love. You see, his marriage hasn't worked properly for ages. And now he's met me and it seems –' and here she would pause for a couple of seconds – 'well, his passion for me scorns mere legal boundaries.'

But Thandiwe was preoccupied these days, cranky, even, flying off the handle when Joanne reminded her that she wanted to borrow her glittery purple nail polish. 'I haven't brought it!' Thandiwe snapped. 'I haven't got time to remember stuff like that.' Or she'd be mouthing off at poor old Miss Dougmore, talking back in class, slamming out the door the second the bell began to ring. 'Ja, Miss, it won't happen again, OK?' Joanne heard her mumble as she passed the two of them in the corridor. 'Exam pressure. Home pressure. Just taking a bit of, you know, *strain*.'

Joanne, too, was taking a bit of strain. There were so many new rules that she had to remember. Etienne insisted that she delete every single one of his texts for safety, even the precious first one that had so swamped her heart with joy. *Pretty baby*, it had run. *I want to kiss u more & moer. Missing u ;) ;) ;)*. He insisted that they part well before six thirty every evening, the time that her father got home from the surgery, even though, as she kept reminding Etienne, her record was so embarrassingly spotless that Dad would believe any excuse she contrived. But Etienne wouldn't budge, merely smiling at her with his cat's eyes half shut and remarking that it would be best if she left the security arrangements up to him. And so he'd drop her at the end of her road on the dot of six fifteen, and she'd run down the pavement to her own front door, almost fainting from the glory of it all.

She'd never been called a woman before. Etienne was the first to do that, and tell her he couldn't stop thinking about her, and present her with a cellophane bag of bittersweet black chocolates, one for every year of her life. No one had ever daubed her initials on a steamed-up car windscreen and then, with those same fingers, moistened the outline of her lips. No one had ever kissed her in a way that made her weak, his tongue first lazy, then thuggish – a skill she supposed, with a protesting clench of the heart, was down to long experience. And unlike the boys she'd gone to school parties with, he seemed so very interested in everything she said. She told him about her classmates; the name of her teacher, Beth Dougmore ('Death Bugmore. Imagine that being your nickname for generations!'). She showed him the poem she'd had published in the school magazine, a twenty-two-verse soliloquy about a pregnant Iraqi woman mistakenly shot dead by US marines, all from the foetus's point of view – not her best effort, actually, but then the editors had probably been relieved to get anything that wasn't about breaking up or ponies.

'So why did you write it?'

'Oh, you know. Just something I was thinking about at the time.'

He'd pressed her hand and gazed at her. He said hell, but it was incredible the way she thought so deeply about what was going on in the outside world, and with a great wave of gratitude she suddenly realised that he *knew* – that he'd pierced right through to the heart of her. That he really understood how difficult it all was. How life wrong-footed you the whole time. How you couldn't just think or do what you wanted, now you were no longer a child. That instead, there was always this horror of letting everyone see that you didn't know what to do with yourself half the time, and that the shameful business of not knowing was all too obvious to every passer-by. Not to mention the hideousness, the humiliation of having being left stranded for so long without a boyfriend, a freakish man-scarer, too clever by half and fit for nothing but passing exams.

And now? Now her revision work would have to wait. She preferred to kiss Etienne on a tucked-away stone bench in the Botanical Gardens, where hardly anyone ever ventured. She preferred to sip Appletisers with him in the deserted lounge of the Stone Crescent Motel under the melancholy gaze of a mounted springbok head, a cigarette stuffed between its jaws. Sometimes, they drove the thirty kilometres to wild and windy Kasouga Beach, avoiding the big summer colony at Port Alfred, where the world and his wife, Etienne said, would be out catching a tan. And they ate takeaway chips with curry sauce in the car on Mountain Drive – sharing swigs from Etienne's bottle of beer as they watched the sun go down behind the town.

When it was time to go he might turn on the car radio and start humming along to the song, looking at her sideways with that little smile he had. 'Riding along in my automobile ... my baby beside me at the wheel ...' he sang, and every time, as the silver car streaked through the lengthening shadows, she would wish that she could stay inside this moment forever. She'd close her eyes and imagine once again how it would be with the two of them naked, his clean fingertips on her skin, whispering that she was special, that he'd known it ever since the first day he saw her, that everything was going to be alright. His arms would fold her into him and because they were in love, she would feel safe. He would whisper that it was their special secret, that what had happened was in no way her fault. He would call her his queen.

On the last day of school before the holidays, Thandiwe told Joanne that her father was leaving home to live with an intern from the ANC office where he was an MP. 'She's the daughter of one of his comrades from the Island,' Thandiwe said as they walked down the hill to the bus station. 'She used to babysit me, for God's sake.' Joanne waited as Thandiwe blew her nose wetly on a crumpled tissue. 'He's found himself this crummy little flat above the public library,' Thandiwe said, her voice loud and harsh. 'He told my mother he needs time to think things through.' She stared at her fingernails, then turned to Joanne. 'She's only four years older than I am. He says they're in love.'

Joanne looked down at her feet. Etienne's wife was going on a trip to visit her family in Port Elizabeth. That morning, Etienne had called Joanne to say he'd decided to drive her there and spend the night. When he got back on Sunday – and here he had paused – they could be alone together for the whole afternoon. They could go all the way together for the very first time. If she could make the arrangements. If she felt for him like she said she did. Like he kept telling her, she had made him need her, and now his need was very great. The thing was, Etienne said, he didn't know how much more waiting he could take.

'But what if the two of them are really in love?' she ventured.

'Joanne, sometimes it's like you're from another planet.' Thandiwe's mouth was twisted and her eyes glistened. 'For her, it's like a career move. She knows she's breaking up a family but she doesn't care. She's a dirty little whore, and soon the whole world will know it too.'

Biting her lip, Joanne withdrew all her birthday money from the ATM before squashing the notes into her Hello Kitty purse and snapping it shut. Saturday had started out unsettled – sultry, but with an ominous build-up of clouds – and now there was a wash of rain on the bank's tall windows. People coming in to queue at the tills were already soaked, so she lingered in the lobby in case the weather cleared, but it did not.

Maybe it was meant to be. As she pressed the catch on her blue umbrella, she thought that maybe the rain would rinse away her stupid fears and stiffness, so by the time she and Etienne met tomorrow she would be ready, equal to anything, and he would like the look of her, love it, even, and nothing would spoil his feast. Shivering from the touch of a stray drop at the nape of her neck, she walked to Birch's department store.

'Do you have this in a small?' she asked the saleslady, pointing to a black basque with stiffly pointed bra cups.

She had no clear idea of the kind of things Etienne might fancy, but she pretended to examine the lingerie section with a wife's disdain.

Playsuits, thongs and something called a shaping suspender. Many of these items had been torn open, then crammed back into their boxes in the heaped display bin. The better stuff floated from a rack ranged beside the fitting room. Silk kimonos. Seamed stockings. Slips in ice-cream-coloured tulle, trimmed with tiny feathers like puffs of fairy breath.

She was stroking a ruffle between her fingers when she felt a tap on her shoulder. She snatched her hand away from the rack as if she'd been stung. In his bulky yellow raincoat with zipped pockets and his brown checked trousers, Doctor Gordon loomed before her, a thin smile hovering above his greying beard. Years ago, when she'd still needed babysitting, he'd been one of a handful of family friends who sometimes helped out; Uncle Gordon, she'd called him then.

'Well, now, Joanne,' the doctor said. 'Christmas shopping, hey?'

'That's right,' she agreed. But then she added, recklessly, 'Shopping for me, actually. A few little numbers for my collection!'

After that, all she could do was hurtle on.

'Right now it's a toss-up between this Paula "skirtini" set, or a "Shirley of Hollywood" basque. Anything you'd recommend?'

He told her a joke involving a woman wearing a pair of foam rubber falsies that accidentally caught fire in an ashtray. He never would have come out with that kind of thing before.

She laughed, but felt her face and neck flush.

'Now you have a happy Christmas, doctor, if Dad and I don't see you before,' she said, much too loudly, still in the new, shrilly flirtatious tone. But the only answer he made was to turn and cast her a look before hurrying on past towards the street.

Moron. Idiot. *Child.* In Birch's washroom, Joanne pressed her face against the mirror and squeezed her eyes tight shut.

A few little numbers for my collection.

She knew the dreadful shyness she felt about her body often

drove her into contortions. She often longed to be less prudish, more relaxed – more like almost every other girl she knew. But she always got shy, way ahead of any reason to get shy. Maybe she was thinking about sex too much; maybe that was why she felt such unease. But when men stared at her breasts that way it seemed that they were helping themselves to her most private self; that self which, until Etienne, she had preferred to keep out of reach.

Even with Etienne she felt the same terrible anxiety, although in the beginning it hadn't seemed to matter that much. 'We will go at your pace, my baby,' was what he had said back then. He wanted so badly to be the first man in her life, and she longed to please him, but behind the longing lurked her problem and it wouldn't go away. And yet more and more frequently she was tormented by thoughts of his wife, always there in the background like a dreadful Christmas tree, aglow with gimcrack, winking charm.

Now Etienne was mentioning more often how he much he needed her, and showing his unpredictable side as well. Oh, yes, he could be moody. Impatient, even; darkening suddenly, then relenting, but only to an air of temporary goodwill, as if he were waiting for a chance to catch her out.

Ja, no, well fine, he said, when she explained she needed good grades to become a doctor like her dad, but the simple truth was that there was work males did better than females and work females did better than males and to think differently was just mist in the sun. Hell, but young people nowadays were spoiled, he told her, when he heard about her plans to study abroad. They had everything handed to them on a plate. He hadn't had anything handed to him on a plate. His father's word had been law, and he had not thought it necessary to give Etienne the opportunity to become educationally up to date.

'You think it's going to be any better for you, Joanne? You and your educated friends; you think you can ignore what this country's all about, that you got it all coming? Let me tell you, my girl, that bunch of bloody mamparas that's in charge now, lining their pockets and their pals' pockets – you mean nothing to them. Meanwhile, the Afrikaner can only sit by while everything is stripped from us.'

He turned to face her, his lips compressed. He usually wore a smooth, cheerful expression, but at these moments he looked as if something heavy and hard was rising up inside him, a blunt wedge of bafflement and rage.

But the desire he'd taught her. Again, that new, tiger-fanged delight leaped through her, striping her with its shocking force. She trusted its power, she craved it; it made her feel like someone, replacing the wobbly fear that nothing really mattered. It had bound her to him with a speed that took her breath away; trusting it, she had leapfrogged the world with him into what felt like the shaky madness of a dream.

And suddenly she wasn't worried any more and all her bad feelings fled. She combed her fringe over the place on her forehead where pimples sprouted, she applied lipgloss with the press of his mouth in mind. A tiny orange spider sat on the mirror's rim, a tack with eyelash legs. Averting her eyes, she scraped it up and bit down fast; it burned a little acrid as she swallowed, a rusty spike, something strong inside of her that would take a good long time to fade.

On Sunday morning, Joanne woke at first light. She scrubbed herself in the shower and rubbed her limbs with cream. She tweezed blonde stubble from her calves and thighs. She crouched on the toilet and then, gripped by a fear that her body stank, went back beneath the shower again. She couldn't relax. The night had passed in a restless dream, the faces of her school friends, of Etienne, the shape of her own sweaty bed in the dark, the sour recesses of her skin, the sound of the clock ticking a torment to her. In a few hours, nothing would be the same.

She had thought she could drag out the rest of the time by reading, but she could not concentrate. Her father called her to the kitchen table for a boiled egg with buttered-toast soldiers but she could not look at him, or eat. The sun was out, but whenever she went into the garden the light hurt her buzzing head. In desperation she walked up the road to Thandiwe's house and knocked on the door.

A housemaid led her into the big white living room with its glass-topped coffee table and expensive-looking chandeliers. Thandiwe and her mother were still at church, the woman said, but they wouldn't be long. She offered Joanne a Diet Coke, which she accepted with shaking hands.

Joanne avoided looking at the giant colour photograph on the wall. She knew that it was Thandiwe's mother and father, posing stiffly in their Xhosa wedding robes. Instead, she stared out of the window, where a gardener with a long-handled cleaning net scratched lines across the watery forehead of the long blue swimming pool.

As she gazed, she imagined the arguments Thandiwe must have overheard in this room. 'After all we've been through?' her mother would have wept. 'What have I done to deserve this?'

Her father's replies would have been embarrassed, gruff. He'd have been trying to calm her down.

'You cheat!' Thandiwe's mother would have raged at him. 'Have you no shame? She's practically our daughter's age!' And then, screaming, 'How could you have sex with a child?'

Joanne, too, felt like screaming. For a crazy instant, she saw herself on the ground, clasping Thandiwe's mum by the ankles and sobbing out an excuse. She tried to deaden her mind, but she knew the image of the wedding photograph wouldn't go away. It made her feel how she once felt when she'd shoplifted a *Vogue* magazine and the store owner had seen her do it. She remembered the look on her father's face when he'd come to pick her up, like he'd been punched in the gut.

She got up quickly and let herself out.

Joanne had thought that Etienne might take her to his place as his wife was away, but to her surprise he did not. He headed for Mountain Drive, where he opened his trousers and, without looking at her, sank himself deep between her thighs with a rapid, grunting twist.

It was all over very quickly, and so different from their usual sessions on the mountainside. Before, he'd talked and she'd listened, and then they would start to kiss and to stroke, her fierce, guilty battle between panic and glutting euphoria rising and falling there on the car's front seat.

This time, Etienne let out a long, hissing sigh.

'Hell's bells, man,' he said. 'You joking with me, Joanne? This your idea of a joke?'

Hell's bells. He loves me now, she thought confusedly, smoothing down her camisole. The knee that was nearest to Etienne touched some part of his own flesh as she shifted closer towards him again.

'But … because like, you never put me in the picture, Joanne. When you said about how you'd never been with a man before and stuff like that, I must've misunderstood.'

Joanne noticed she had goosebumps on her arms and chest. Her father was planning on buying her a white leatherette jacket for passing her exams. She'd checked the computer and seen that he'd looked at one in an online store. But she'd gone all to pieces in the exams. Towards the end, she'd hardly bothered studying. English, usually her favourite, had been the worst. She'd blanked out completely during composition and couldn't even fill one page.

Etienne was still speaking, his mouth working in that odd way that made his words come out choked. With an effort, she concentrated. He was saying that he'd had quite a few doubts about going this far with her, but jirre, for what?

It's OK, she said, trying to sound normal again. Doesn't change us, does it? She smiled at him, just as if he'd told her a really clever joke.

'I'm crazy about you, my girl,' Uncle Derek used to whisper, the afternoons when he was babysitting and he'd wake her up from her nap. His little treasure, he'd breathe, saying also that he was old enough to be her father but that he had just got carried away. Time and again he'd say he was so sorry.

So maybe now he should just forget about the lovey-dovey stuff, Etienne was saying, and just do whatever the hell. Because he couldn't help feeling he'd been misled.

It was Uncle Derek who said she was his secret, his and his alone, and then that the whole world would know what a dirty little cunt she was if she ever told.

Joanne looked at Etienne's shiny brass belt-tip, hanging heavy against the massive curve of his thigh. She wanted him to turn towards her in the silence that had come, to reach out and put a hand on her arm. But he would not look at her. She tilted her head back against the passenger door so she could see outside.

It was almost sunset, she noticed – that strange moment when the veld drains to the dead colour of a cold roast, just before the pinks and reds come streaking in. Through the windscreen, she glimpsed the dark tops of the bitter aloes and the stinkwood trees. Soon, lamps would be coming on in the streets below. What you going to do, anyway, hey – call a cop? Etienne was saying, as he moved towards her again, but she felt strangely weightless; if she concentrated hard enough, she might simply float out of the window and away. Yes, that was something she could do; she would hover near the silver car in the warm air above the mountainside, a quick, hopeful, pulsing bead of light. And then she'd be gone, flying off to where his eyes could not follow her, over the wide night sky that was stretched across the town.

The Chameleon House

*Their eyes gave out an eager spirited light that
resembled near-genius, but was youth merely.*
– Muriel Spark, *The Girls of Slender Means*

Ever watched a chameleon backed into a corner? They turn black
with rage. Slowly, of course, but with a strange ferocity, the dark
impulse unfurling over that scaly body like a sombre flag. And all
the while they're keeping tjoepstil, those dot eyes staring in their
crazy turret sockets, one checking ahead, the other behind. You'll
stare too for a while, because there's always a weird kind of glamour
in confrontation, even with a lizard, until it gets bored or you do. You
might think about telling the ragged kid with the stick or whoever's
doing the tormenting to stop prodding the creature, to let it alone,
but most probably you walk on by. There are bigger troubles to deal
with in the world.

That's the way it was with Dena and me. The summer I lived in
London with her I came to see her like that – frightened, stripped
of her camouflage and cornered while the rest of us watched. She
and I, Karen and Tracy, we'd all left South Africa for the first time
that year and even with the glare and roar of a massive new city to
negotiate, we were always greedy for something more. So every day

we ran, desperate to keep up, from gigs and parties and underground raves to the indie boutiques for those grunge threads all the hipsters wore then, always with a portable stereo roaring out Hugh Masekela or the Happy Mondays parked on the end of our beds.

Plus I had other issues, strung out on TJ, my man from back home. I was a liability at work, forgetting change, dropping glasses, yelling at the chefs when my orders went through slow. Nearly got fired for it a couple of times, but I would almost have welcomed that. It was hard to focus on anything much.

I wasn't the only one with a rubbish job. All four of us cadged whatever cash we could – we'd come into the country on holiday visas, no official right to work. Dena scrubbed offices for the White Glove Cleaning Agency in Hammersmith; she'd been there five or six months already by the time we turned up. We joked she must be scrubbing away her white-girl guilt – most people only stuck it out a matter of weeks. Yet she worked longer hours than any of us, turning up her Walkman, squeegeeing and vacuuming, claiming the routine lulled her into a kind of trance. She learned to hold her breath scraping the ammonia crusts off the urinals, she told us, and prising those clotted plaits of slime and hair from the plugs of blocked-up sinks. And she learned to hide how good she'd got at it because if the boss found out, he cut down on your hours to save himself a buck.

We liked it, this city full of restless passers-through like ourselves. The four of us rented a place together in Collingwood Road, a cramped, litter-strewn street lined with terraced houses whose bulging windows gave them the air of fat men wearing waistcoats buttoned too tight. At night I lay in bed and listened to our Polish neighbour knocking about, watching TV game shows and muttering. Like Karen and Tracy, who shared the sitting room, and Dena, in the box-room at the back, I was always broke, but that was supposed to be part of the whole experience, right? So a couple of days a week I waitressed at Café Koha, while weekends I worked in a pub near Chinatown. I spent the other nights bar-hopping or just getting out of it with whoever happened to be in the house at the time.

No matter how wasted I got, I always seemed to wake when the clock radio would be going off in the Joburg flat, with TJ yawning his way out of bed and feeling sleepily for his jeans, and outside the quivering fingers of the bougainvillea vine stroking the window in the pearly light.

We all knew each other from student days, but Dena and us, we were never that tight. She had had her own crowd back then, and anyway she was reserved; someone with high walls, you know? But now, in her own aloof way, she seemed just as determined to remake herself as the rest of us. Wednesday night was what we called our girls' night out, cocktails and calamari at El Metro in Hammersmith tube station in our new grunge gear and piercings, London-style, while we debated which clubs and drugs we could afford. When we were really skint, we cadged free drinks off a guy Tracy was seeing. He worked the bar at Club Afrique, this basement off the Strand where fixers and go-getters from all over the continent sipped beer and studied the crowd with shining, attentive eyes.

Dena never really let go, though; never got along with the lines of cheap speed and the partying and the pretending to be wild. I kissed her once in some bar late at night, to get rid of a drunk who wouldn't let her alone. I leaned over and kissed her on the mouth, softly but firmly, a long kiss, my hand in her hair, and afterwards she couldn't look me in the eye, although her admirer disappeared without saying another word. She tasted like me – beer and cigarette smoke, plus some odd, sour back note I couldn't quite define. It was rare that she stayed the course, but if she was still around at three in the morning I thought – in the beginning, at least – that it was easy to see what she really was, a nice Afrikaner doedie; sturdy, like most farm girls, in unobjectionable clothes, blonde hair scraped back, laughing politely on cue but always watchful from under her hooded eyes. Efficiently sorting out the taxi home and the house keys as the rest of us stood on the kerb, yelling drunkenly in the street lamps' dirty yellow light.

Still, she stuck around with us because we were cool; at least, we flattered ourselves that we were back then. God knows she needed fun; Dena had been through some tough times. She'd been *involved* – that's what we called it then; part of a network of student activists who'd linked up with the underground movement in exile. No child's play, my china, with thousands of people getting arrested on public violence charges or jailed without trial, and many others beaten, tortured or shot. Eventually, the security police tracked her down in hiding and took her to Port Elizabeth, where she spent just short of four months in the North End jail. She hardly spoke of it, but she told me once that her parents never visited her there. For them, her involvement was a crossing point, a tribal betrayal. Her people were godsdienstige, Dena said; they took the narrow road.

She gave me an ornamental chameleon once, strung with dark blue beads. The kind that street kids make from copper wire. Me and TJ, we had a whole collection of those wire toys in the flat, starfish and bicycles, even a little train, and I told her one time I missed having them around.

For you, she said. So you can start a new hoard. Got it down by PE beachfront, she said. Day they let me out. Couldn't think where to go for a while, so I took the bus and just parked off there by Summerstrand. Watched the moms playing with their kids, the seagulls flocking, ate the best ice cream I'd ever tasted. I had four of them, one after the other! Guy selling them thought I was mal, or high. That country, hey.

TJ and me loved the sea. Liked to camp out on those big, bare Transkei beaches once the rains had come and gone, heading as far north as we could hack it in the 4x4 to where it gets so lush and wild you can stop wearing clothes for days because there's no one around to see. We'd planned to get married up there, throw a big party in Port St Johns, at the Rhodes Hotel. Got the invitations drafted and all. Left my ma to deal with all that stuff; just walked away from it and she never asked what or why. No doubt she had her views.

TJ couldn't get over why I'd done what I did. Listen, it meant nothing. I got out of it one night and pulled an action, I told him. Trying to make him smile, using that old Durban surfer slang he grew up with, but he didn't smile.

He was my man, had been since I was seventeen, and I never meant to do him down. But don't we all do stupid stuff that's no good for you? You do it and afterwards you find there's no going back or feeling relaxed about it or anything like that.

In five years together we'd only spent a month apart, when he went home to Durban after his dad died. The day he got back he spent an age slashing away at the bougainvillea covering the front wall of our flat, trickling its tendrils over the windows and turning the room inside mermaid green. I told him, TJ, leave it, I like the way it falls; it makes our place private, a secret cave we can hide out in. He said no, what we needed was to keep tearing the damn stuff down. He said it's easier than you think to get hooked on living a secret life.

Check this out, half-price deals to Ibiza, Dena said at one of our Wednesday night sessions. We were reading the *Evening Standard*'s travel section out loud, wincing every time the barroom door banged open and a rainy wind blew in. It was early June. The movies paint a picture of these strawberry-filled English summers, with never a hint of how sodden they actually are. We were always fantasising about which foreign beaches we were going to blow our hard-earned bucks on, to try and get warm.

Ja, but a hundred and fifty pounds more gets you to Thailand, where it's thirty degrees right now. This was Tracy, gingerly turning her new nose-stud as she scanned the room. Catch a full moon party on Ko Phangan, dance all night, they say it's like meditation in action. Fully, man. A month there'll sort out all our shit.

I can so picture you there – that place will be perfect for your kind of vibe, my koeks, nodded Dena, with a gracious tilt of the head. We watched as she sipped her beer, waiting until she'd swallowed, replacing her glass right in the middle of the stained beer mat. All three of us had plenty to say, but we waited until Dena said her quiet word first and then jumped in. I thought of the queues that sprouted in shops and outside clubs in this sober northern city, static conga-lines that always seemed so tidy and well-behaved. People here swerved into line like it was a duty; now suddenly we were swerving behind Dena's words in much the same way. It was remarkable, you know, how quickly she took that role away from me, and without even missing a beat.

But that night Karen had something on her mind, and she was all lit up with it.

Listen, Dena. Grant phoned.

Karen's brother. A nice guy, with struggle credentials good enough to net him a reporter's job with the newly beefed-up state broadcaster.

Ja, there's this new documentary coming up, perfect for you. Free tickets home to do an interview and maybe a fee.

Hmm, what – activist stuff? Because, you know, all that's kind of behind me now. Dena pulled a demure face, but she looked pleased.

Of course, said Karen, nodding admiringly. Karen revered Dena like she had the power of healing. It was embarrassing to see – maybe she was hoping some of that I-suffered-with-the-comrades karma would transfer itself to suburban old her. My toes curled for her sometimes, really they did. She pulled her chair closer, her face all stern.

This one's big budget. You know how the government's going public with the old secret police records? So the idea is to film activists from the struggle days checking out their files! All those search-and-destroy dirty tricks, Dena, how the apartheid government harassed the comrades fighting for justice, here's your chance to expose what they did to you! To the world!

Star in a film? asked Tracy, bright-eyed. Nice one, man. Wonder if I've got a police file.

Searched at a roadblock once, weren't you, my sweet? Dena said, quickly. This time, her smile wasn't quite lighting up her face.

Oh my God! That bonehead cop …

I pressed my lips together to stifle a giggle. We'd only heard this story about a dozen times.

… old as my grandad, patting my arse every which way, siestog man! Must be his worst nightmare to be a policeman with the Rainbow Nation, if he's even still got a job.

You bet. Listen, let's drink to that. And Dena was gone, shouldering through the crowd to buy another round.

By nine thirty the room was filling up, bodies jostling, everyone gulping the drinks down, sweating and smoking, hot and loud. At times like this, with a kind of liquid hilarity rippling through the room, London seemed the best place in the world. We could be anyone, taking a punt on a new style or image; no one would slap you down. At first, we had been reluctant to say where we were from – we were ashamed to be lumped in with all those old crooks and killers in the apartheid regime. But it wasn't long before we realised that people didn't seem to care about any of that. In fact, they looked the other way if you brought it up. Try and explain to a Brit why you didn't think things had really changed that much back home – that where you came from, your mom and dad arse-kissed their colleagues at work but still called them 'kaffirs' round the dinner table, and eight times out of ten they'd just cough politely and look blank. Most people seemed quite keen on the idea that the worst was over and everything was now pretty much on track; it was somehow rather tedious for them to be called upon to speculate on whether that old apartheid corpse had simply been shoved in a corner and left to rot. And that was fine for us too. For us, it was a relief beyond telling to fit in so easily, like now in this long slow mash-up of music and talking and lights, everything going trippy as you touched it, smooth and warm like love.

Tracy's voice cut through a lull. She was laughing at Karen who was bumping about on all fours, plump calves twinkling in the gloom. She'd lost an earring, one of a pair of mine. Big, look-at-me earrings, gorgeous, but fake – just gritty flecks of marcasite.

In the blue-tiled ladies' room, Dena leaned over the basin and held something up to her face until the mirror danced with shards of light. In the right light she looked arresting, much more so than the TV and newspaper images would later suggest, since the camera always underlined a thick-set cast to her features, ignoring the sinuous nature of her hooded eyes, or the way her mood could transform her face. I myself never believed in her more than that night when she found the earring, when I stopped at the door and saw her smile at herself – a private self, wolfishly seductive and strange – and she saw me look, and carried on smiling.

Was that when things between Dena and the rest of us began to go wrong? Because she must have been figuring out her next move by then – the reinvention that was yet to come. Ja, it was about then that something odd took hold of her; something I thought I recognised, but didn't understand. She began to brood, pretending to stay part of the gang without actually being involved. She would giggle automatically at the jokes the rest of us made, keep her hooded eyes down, light another cigarette, gnaw at her nails till they split – anything rather than join in, the way she used to. I remember feeling intrigued at how well she kept it up.

July started out grey and damp, the wettest, they said, since records began. The Saturday the South Africans were scheduled to play at Lords, the rain fell in sheets, shutting us into a pinched and dreary world. All the rooftops echoed with the steady drum of it, and the afternoon grew airless round us like a shell.

Our landlord turned up around six. As usual, he'd brought a bottle of Bombay Sapphire gin, and takeaway pizza in a greasy box. Gulbash Singh was a Glaswegian who talked a lot about the 1980s, his Klondyke years, when he'd been an astrologer to the stars; Princess Di had once paid him a call. Now he spun out a meagre income as Psychic Singh, writing horoscopes for a knitting magazine.

He liked to get drunk with us now and again, usually after he'd had a letter from his ex-girlfriend in Edinburgh – a 'super lady', he called her, who had sun, moon and rising signs all astonishingly compatible with his own. I really love her, he would moan.

Well, why don't you get back together with her, then? I said to him that day. But it wasn't straightforward, it seemed; she was with someone else now, a woman, and they wanted to have a kid. He'd offered to be a sperm donor and she'd just laughed. I'm like, Damn, what is it with you Brits? Do you always have to look on the bright side?

Didn't take long for Karen to fill him in on how her boet, Grant, had scored a luck with this documentary gig, how Singh must persuade Dena to quit being modest and take part. She really pushed it. Everyone who hung out with us had to hear the tale, and every time Dena would look away, ride it out with a tight little smile.

Have a drink with us, Dena, my fierce South African queen, said Singh in his most placatory voice.

Cheers, but I'm about to go out. No expression on that pale, pointed face. She was methodically emptying the drying rack, putting pots and cutlery away.

Dena, Dena, Dena, said Singh cheerfully, munching on a pizza slice. You're turning down this chance to shine, but why?

Plenty of others. They'll do just fine without me.

Ha, ha. Tell me. You were a victim, too, yes? You suffered at the hands of those mule-headed Boers, my child. So put the past to rest! Why not?

Done that already, Mr Singh. By coming out here.

Och, Dena. But now that everything is being swept out into the open over there …

Dena slammed down the pan she was holding and spun around. I'm not needed there any more, she hissed. So leave me the fuck alone, and she ran from the room, banging the door behind her.

It was not her words, exactly, as much as the look on her face that was so startling. Singh stared, his mouth fallen slightly open. For about six long seconds there was no sound but the steady gurgling of the rainwater dripping through an outside drain.

All of a sudden, Singh cleared his throat and pointed to something on the table. Must a man die of thirst in his own house? he said.

His bottle of gin stood on a wicker tray. Karen mixed him another drink and he took a large, thoughtful swig.

Chin, chin, he said, and then: Let me give you a little tip about Dena, my girls.

What?

He took another pull and turned to look at the closed kitchen door. She's not what she seems.

What's that supposed to mean? I said, after a while.

It means, she's not all you think she is, he said, louder this time. Or what Karen's brother thinks she is or anyone else. He had another long swig of the gin. That Scorpio vigour of expression, always so fascinating. She will always be an excitingly unpredictable house-mate, my dear friends. My question is, what is going to occur with the emotional intensity of the coming full moon? Do you promise to keep me fully informed?

With a sigh, I set down my glass. I'd been clenching it, and my knuckles had turned white. Of course, I said. We'll watch carefully for the effects of the moon, Gulbash. We'll keep you fully informed.

Like TJ might say, keeping secrets can become a habit. But even those of us who lived with her couldn't say just how or why Dena first got hooked. For sure, it must have started long before the story the newspaper exposés told, that she spent years as a police spy. Ja, she sold her sob story to the papers right after she ducked back home. August rent money still in her back pocket. Singh was terribly upset.

See, once she knew people were going to start combing those police files, they'd soon work out who'd been ratting on who. So she must have seen a bust coming. Running off to London was just one way of putting off the inevitable. One side or the other, they didn't give a damn about her.

Anyway, Dena told the journalists that she started informing at school, final year. Her English teacher had a brother – some big shot cop – who recruited her. She kept going when she got to varsity, where the bucks the white government offered helped pay her fees. She never went to jail. In the end, she got too frightened to stop because her handlers said they'd blow her cover. I was manipulated, she said. I'd give anything to undo what happened, anything. That's what she told them.

Picked her moment, I'll give her that. The country awash with truth and reconciliation and all that. And of course, she found a way to adapt, once the fuss died down. My ma heard she's started up a job placement agency in Johannesburg, finding cleaners for the new black elite. Few things show you've made it like getting someone else in to do the dirty work – that's something all South Africans understand, you know? And that's what Dena was sharp enough to see.

People say, but there must have been clues. Amazing, you didn't guess a thing! And I just smile and say, well, there was a lot going on.

But the clues were there.

I met this guy at a party, right before I left for London. A few weeks later, I went round to his flat in Yeoville and lay with him on his sagging bed, listening and then not listening to the noise of people shouting at the far end of the passage. When I opened my eyes, this is what I saw: his nipples, like apple pips. Our bodies – one white, one brown – joined together. His frowning face as he came.

Three weeks, it took me to build up to that – three weeks of sleepless nights, of burning, of failing nerves; of learning to juggle the burning with the cold-blooded business of getting the damn thing going. Messages, movements, meeting-places: all needed secret negotiation, like spies struggling to protect some tiny, doomed state. Still, I worked it all out, how I'd behave when I came home to TJ and our big sad bed, fingers still wiped with that cheating smell, pumped with my stolen power. Trying all the time not to think about how the other guy had clearly gone through all this before – he knew the ropes.

Afterwards, he saw me back to my car, all the terrors of the Joburg night slinking back into the shadows as we roared down the stairs together, enormous, blazing. We'd had a smoke, we were very high. Couple of times walking through the car park I miscalculated my width, scraping into a bin, and the back of a blue BMW. TJ was waiting for me, arms folded across that faded T-shirt that made his eyes look so blue. The other guy still had his arm around me, one hand touching my breast. I couldn't look as he flinched away. Take it easy, man, he said to TJ. Stammering, hoarse, he was so nervous.

TJ said to me, We'll talk about this at home, and I said, Piss off, and got into the car. Left them to it. Stayed at my ma's that night, came back, listened to what TJ had to say and then I went and booked my plane ticket. Stood in the queue at Departures, hips and legs still splotched with bruises from the BMW. Black pearls. A thief's reward.

You know, I was the last person she spoke to in the house before she left.

I remember it was a Sunday lunchtime. I hadn't heard or seen her all day, so I stuck my head around her bedroom door. Didn't knock. I just knew something was going on.

She was still in her dressing gown, her hands prodding and picking at stray threads on the sash. And there was her big green backpack splayed open on the floor, half-full.

It was always so tidy, that room – scraped neat, no books or balled-up tights or messy jars of make-up, just a hot water bottle hooked behind the door, clean blouse on the narrow chair, and on the wall, a souvenir poster from the Globe Theatre in a curly script:

> *... Love is not love*
> *Which alters when it alteration finds*
> *Or bends with the remover to remove*

I had brought some grapes from the kitchen table, the big, purple kind, and I started to eat them, one by one. I made some crack about Dena's poster, about her being an intellectual beacon in this house of degenerates, and she shrugged and said ja, the guy who taught them English at school, for him Shakespeare was a hero. He'd scared the hell out of them, too. If anyone needed wrestling into line, Mr Engelbrecht had you stand at the front on an upturned wastepaper bin. When the bell rang, he'd make a big play of kicking it out from under you, like he was scoring a drop goal. You little shits need to learn about *respect*, she said, mimicking his accent, her mouth thin and tight.

Eventually I said it looked as though she was packing up.

Ah, she said, colouring a bit. What, me leave our little family?

She went on, But it's worked out well, don't you think? It's been great, us four together.

It was the way she said it, like she was so sure of my answer.

Hope we've provided some entertainment value for you at least, I said. How do we score?

What? she said, after waiting for a while.

How's your mind, Dena, I said. You couldn't care less about our *little family* really, hey? Because you're so clever. Always one step ahead. Always in control. And now I see you're leaving us; perhaps you thought we wouldn't notice. You don't give a damn about us in the house and there's no shame in you at all.

I don't understand, Dena said. Entertainment value? That's good, that's hilarious. Like I'd choose to hang out with you guys, if I didn't have to? I feel sorry for you.

Sorry for us! I said, laughing, like it was funny.

You're all so try-hard, she goes, with your shiny new nose-studs and your Camden Market clothes. But you're still a bunch of spoilt, over-privileged white bitches underneath. Do you even have a game plan for that – for the way you represent, back home? Because you don't fool anyone over here, you know. The only people you manage to impress are other oddballs, like Singh.

I took a deep breath.

Ja, I said. But the world's a bigger place now, Dena. Nobody gives a fuck where the white South Africans end up or what happens to us. But that's not your problem, Dena, is it? Your problem is your real nature is written all over your face and everybody can see it. I can see it. Think you can ever look anyone back home in the eye again, do you, Dena – you cheat?

I was just going with my hunch, but her face, her pale eyes – I can see the hurt there now, as it struggled with surprise. I remember the effort it took to keep my hands from clenching and my breathing slow. *And here's Belinda Mackenzie with Open Book,* said a radio announcer's voice through the wall

Dena kept on staring at me, but now she looked afraid. Then she hid her face in her hands and said, almost in a whisper, Don't look at me that way.

And I heard it at last, a familiar, wrenching sound: the same one, choked and raw, that forced its way out of me late at night as I lay guilty and sleepless in the dark, alone.

I walked off and sat in the kitchen, ate some more grapes.

They tasted both bitter and sweet.

Mask

You open your eyes with a start and peer through the dimness for the thing that woke you. Some kind of greyish, hooded creature – you felt its sleeve brush your cheek. But no one stirs. A hush hangs over everything. You're safe. You're just nodding off again when the man in front begins to snore, a hideous sound – a real, classic sound-turd, and yes, here comes a long line of them, every relentless, stinking one the same; each grunting moistly upwards before pinching itself out in a tiny *ssss*.

You're so tired, you want to wrench off a stiletto and give the man's arse-head a slap he'll never forget, but then you remember why you must not – you must never even think of doing that. Instead, you just make a note of the noise. It reminds you of somebody. Could you remember everyone you slept with, just by the way they snored? You could try to list them that way, in your head. An audio ID parade. You've got to do something to stretch out the time before the plane lands in Johannesburg.

'Michelle! You've awoken.' The Brazilian guy on your aisle side is staring at you. 'Difficult not to, eh, with this terrible man in the front.' His teeth gleam wetly.

You've lied to him that you are Michelle, an exchange student coming home to Joburg from a Sao Paulo language school.

'You know you talk in your sleep, Michelle?'

Sandro. That's his name. *What did I say?* Small and sallow-skinned, with a little bokbaardjie that looks like it's been oiled. He said he was a doctor – well, you pity his patients. The pinkie finger on his right hand has an extra-long, yellowish nail that would give anyone the shivers, not to mention he's been dopping back the brandies since you got on the plane.

'Is it, man? I hope I didn't disturb you too much, Sandro.'

His small yellow hands tremble slightly as they rest on the beige pull-out tray. He picks up his drink and sucks in a slow mouthful.

'Michelle, you were not happy. You were calling somebody some very bad names. In a tone which might, eh, strike the fear of God into anyone's heart. An unexpected performance, you know, from such a lovely young lady – and a young lady, what's more, in the family way.'

He checks you out, his bright eyes unblinking. Fokall to do with you, poes. Since when did being pregnant mean you had to talk lah-di-dah?

'Ja, sorry, Sandro, hey. I'm not used to flying, you know?' You summon a cheerful smile, but suspect it is coming off tight and small.

'Ah, no – no need for regrets, Michelle. But you sounded so very unhappy. I thought to myself: whatever has this beautiful young creature got to be sad about?'

Isn't it just your luck to be saddled with this bokdrol?

'You see, I also noticed, Michelle, that you couldn't understand our stewardess when she asked in Portuguese how you were today. You asked her to translate. That's strange, I thought, for a language student – but then it is also true that Sao Paulo has many temptations to keep a young girl like you away from her studies, eh!' And he raises his glass to you in a mock toast, the signet ring on his horrible pinkie glittering like the eye of an alligator.

You stare at him, frozen.

Ag, calm down for fuck's sake, relax. Just another sad old boykie heading for a hangover; heading to pass out in some failed motel room at the end of the flight.

Draining his drink, Sandro summons a fresh one from a passing trolley.

'Ah, well, now Michelle. Perhaps we are not so very different, you and I. Tell me, do you have an opinion on the age when people are most likely to sin – to stray from the path? Is it likely to be when they are very young, and so gloriously in love with themselves that they think they are heroes and invincible; or later, in the middle of life, in that dark wood, where every day the path ahead grows more and more remorselessly to resemble the one already left behind?'

OK, call the airhostess and get them to move you away from the mad guy. You twist in your seat, but at the same moment the cabin lurches, the air in the jet engines ringing shrill. The plane starts to struggle with unseen assailants out there in the dark. An alarm bell rings. As the captain's voice comes over the intercom, talking cheerily about turbulence, the people around you shift and sigh. Seat belts clink, a sound like gold coins sliding from palm to palm. A child cries out. Wiping your sweaty hands on your jeans, you press your forehead to the window and peer out at the sky.

Long fingers of rain are stroking the glass. Somewhere down there is the Kalahari: what luck! You went all the way to Brazil, but if the plane crashes now, you'll die in the very same shithole you were born in. You wonder if it's raining down there on the farm; fat drops bouncing on thirsty red soil, darkening the leaves of the kiwanos and the camel thorn trees.

You were seven when your family left the Kalahari. Skinny and gap-toothed, and the only girl in your class with a giant tortoise for a pet. Your grandfather drilled a hole in Skillie's shell so she could pull you around on a little sledge. But by the time you'd outgrown the sledge, the Delports' farming days were done, too. By then, years of drought had sucked the life out of everything. The fields all smoky with dust. Even the grass by the dam was brown.

Abraham, the farm manager, helped load up the truck and the old blue Fiat. Watching from the car window, you saw your grandfather raise a hand towards Abraham, as if to pat him on the shoulder, but then he dropped it again and just stood there without speaking. Abraham's brown face was as stiff as your grandfather's white one. As the family's convoy crunched down the drive, Abraham got smaller and smaller, until he was only a tiny dot by the wind pump. Was he watching you, too, become just a small dot in the distance?

You are shaken with a grief for Skillie you had thought was long gone.

'Anything wrong, Michelle?' Sandro leans his sallow face towards you again. The collar of his shirt is frayed. You can smell his yellow breath.

You shrink away, and close your eyes. Your tongue finds the scab on your lip and worries at it.

You are still worrying at it two hours later, as the plane bumps down onto South African soil. Across the terminal's façade, distorted in the plane's convex window, you can see the airport's name. Three letters are gone, the dilapidation a crumb of comfort – slack is part of the way things work round here. You watch as a baggage truck, lights blinking, speeds to the spot where your plane is heading to park. Behind it, two yellow vehicles. Police. Looking for illegal immigrants. Terrorists, even.

Or a girl with a stomach stuffed with cocaine.

The first shock was that the promised beachfront hotel never materialised. But the big house they took you to instead was so beautiful, you didn't care. Zé, tall in his steel-tipped cowboy boots, picked you up from the airport and gave you a glimpse of your first foreign city, patches of colour flying past like hallucinations. A neon-winking Christ on a giant billboard, arms outstretched. Jacarandas, plumbago and hibiscus everywhere, just like home. Police with big guns. Even a sprawling township, right near the rich neighbourhood where the villa was.

Once the first thrill of being there had drained away, each day began to feel like part of the one before, only connected to the rest by your complicated dreams. You spent your time by the pool, eating prego rolls and staring up at the clear January sky. Ringing for take-out, whatever you wanted: pizza with steak toppings, stir-fry or chicken stew. Your biggest decision was how to blow the money they gave you up-front, because they wouldn't let you go near the tall electronic gates. In the end, you told Zé what you wanted and he bought it: a leather jacket from a big department store, something you'd seen in *Vogue Brasil*. Champagne coloured, like your hair. With the buttons done up, you could hardly see your bump.

Would he miss you at all? Zé, with his woolly knitted cap and eyes like licked caramels. You saw how he checked you out as you walked around your sunlounger, more aware than ever of how the soft swell of your belly made your hips sway. You were pleased the bump had stayed so small; even now, with twenty-nine weeks gone, it's still like that. At night, he had stuck around to watch the soaps with you, laughing at the telenovela he liked best, at the complicated things that happened to Tiao, the rodeo cowboy, and Creuza, the lustful woman who pretended to be shy. Despite not knowing the language, you had understood everything that went on between them. With Zé, it was a different story. You knew that he liked you, but in all those days together, he never so much as touched your hand.

The next shock came on the fifth day, when Zé turned up with a laptop and a woman called Giselle. Big breasted, hard faced, in your bedroom she chopped out lines on the dog-eared TV guide, looking faintly surprised when you refused. She spread the contents of the laptop case onto your pink floral sheet: the pill so you wouldn't go to the toilet on the plane; the Chloraseptic spray, to loosen up your throat; finally, the cocaine – half a kilo in twenty-eight condom-wrapped pellets, each the size of your thumb. 'Swallow, no chew, see?' Giselle explained, throwing her head back and demonstrating, her throat supple and brown against the whiteness of her T-shirt. 'Two, yes? Every twenty minutes. Take your time, easy, nice.'

Even now, thinking of your baby floating in its warm, clean sac with all that stuff so near it makes you feel sick and faint. You stammered that there'd been a mistake – a big one. That Femi told you you'd bring the package home in the lining of a bag. There was a nasty moment of silence. Zé stopped shifting the match he'd been chewing from one side of his mouth to the other, his face suddenly very still. Finally, Giselle forced a smile. '*Mama pequena*, little momma,' she cooed in a voice bright as a broken bottle, 'no one will suspect a pregnant woman! Much safer than inside a suitcase.' When you cried she slapped your face, her gold rings beading your lip with blood. 'OK, so we keep you here and you never go home,' she said. 'You want your money, white girl? Then work for it. Does anyone at your house even know where the fuck you are?'

They sat with you for the next five hours, while you swallowed. Feeding you sips of water from a toothbrush glass. About half-way through, when your dry-retching wouldn't stop, Giselle rummaged in her bag for a half-full bottle of massage oil; you shut your eyes and pretended it was medicine. They explained again how the rest of it would work. How when you got to Joburg, someone would be waiting for you at the airport. You'd go to another hotel, take another pill, wait for it all to come out. It could take a couple of days, they said. After that, you'd get paid.

And now there are police at the airport, before the plane has even stopped. What made you too stupid to understand that Zé and Giselle would lie? For sure there'd be another girl in the villa this week, wide-eyed and wondering at the easy luxury, at the satellite TV and the surround-sound stereo system. Were you being punished for getting upset? Did Zé call the cops? Maybe your arrest would cause a useful commotion, so that some other girl with a bigger stash could slip by unseen. Ag, what a fool you are, so dumbly trusting and slow.

Ma. You have a sudden, desperate longing to see your mother's face. The night before you left, you'd met at the flat in Vanderbijlpark. Bertus had been giving her a hard time, she told you – drinking, ranting about respect, grabbing Ma's greying plait, pushing that big face of his with its starbursts of broken blood vessels up close to Ma's worn one. But she smiled at you, her suikerbos. She stroked your hair. You smiled back, but you hadn't been able to look Ma in the eye. You couldn't face the intensity of that frightened, watery gaze, those eyes diluted with a sadness that seeped into your very bones.

You and Ma, you knew, would not meet again for a long while, not after this. Ma, clinging to the old days, recognising nothing in the politicians' rainbow nation, would never understand where the money had come from, or how far you had fallen – and how far you were still prepared to go. That there was nothing you would not now do to lift yourself and the child beyond the limits of Vanderbijlpark and seize a stake in the larger world. You had so many things to take care of, and it made you tired and weak and aching on the inside. A farm dried out by desert dust. Your fields on fire. The air all filled with smoke, and Ma never seemed to see.

Fool, blerrie fool. But Charnay, you are something special, Zé had said. You look like an angel; you are carrying a child. They will check out your passport, they will see – *Dios Mio!* she's only seventeen. You are not what the cops look out for; no way. No problem at all for you to go into that airport and come out the other side.

He was probably smiling at you as he said it, but you could not take your eyes from the bed. Some massage oil had puddled on the laptop case, and it was giving off such dazzling, tantalising reflections.

'Let us in, man! We're good South Africans. We like rugby and we all drink beer.' A big guy in sunglasses and a green sports shirt is joking with the official at the immigration booth up ahead. The airport only has a skeleton staff. A public sector strike is in full swing, but extra police have been drafted in, a hoarse voice announces over the tannoy, so that security 'will not be compromised'. But everything is moving at an agonisingly slow pace.

'Just be patient, sir, and we'll try and get this sorted for you as quickly as we can.' At the head of your queue, a woman in a long gown and a scarf wrapped turban-style around her head is arguing over a piece of paper. Soon it will be your turn. It has taken almost an hour, and finally you are approaching the front of the line. Yet before this queue had even moved a step, you started feeling it – a pang of heat nudging through your body, the upwelling of a small, red pain.

You are trying to ignore it. Zé told you these were good-quality condoms – the best – but you need to treat them with respect. Don't eat or drink on the plane. And you must stay cool. Acid from an angry stomach can melt the plastic and then … he'd shaken his head. Big trouble. Someone he'd known once, a Rio woman, had got an overdose after a condom burst in her stomach while she was flying back from Lima. She'd drunk a ginger beer, then fallen down, saying she was all on fire. They rushed her to hospital, he said, as soon as the plane landed, but it was too late. It had taken her six days to die.

Your turn. Stepping forward, you feel the new bad feeling again, only now it is worse.

'Goeie môre, meneer. How are you?' Your voice is steady, but you can feel sweat burning on your forehead and the backs of your knees. The heat from your gut envelopes you, then slowly sinks away.

A policeman with a sniffer dog is idly circling the queue. You have practised this part a thousand times. You will not give yourself away by any change of expression or sudden movement. On your face there is a perfectly even smile. After telling the official what he wants to know, you will continue walking at a steady pace; past the dog that is waiting to sniff at you, waiting to get at the smell of your betrayal. You'll stroll into the arrivals hall, alive with the warmth of families, their bundles and exclaiming relatives. Then you'll be home.

'Sawubona, welcome to Jozi. And where have you come from this morning?'

You give him an even bigger smile. That's an easy one. You begin to answer, but find you can't remember the words. Instead, the pain is back again, the pain that is forcing itself open in your stomach and clutching at your throat. And your heart is pounding loudly, making you feel dizzy and faint. You lick your lips, conscious of the officer with the dog coming up behind you on the left-hand side. Everything seems to have gone still.

The official is looking at you expectantly, ballpoint pen poised. A queer sense of calm courses through you as you lower your head to your hands, resting your forehead against the booth's dusty glass. You are drifting away, feeling firm hands warm on your shoulders, the fragment of a bad dream – a greyish, hooded creature scraping the seeds from a swollen sunflower – finally fading. This, after all, is the real tempo of life, you realise, as with an almost unbearable slowness every second stretches out until it almost stops, and all movement turns to stone. In the heat and the clamour, a whistle blows, someone shouts, a dog whines. But your grandfather is pulling you towards him, stroking your forehead and holding you fast against his chest, and at last you are able to sleep.

You are rich with Friday-night wages and there are swallows dipping and soaring in the mild October sun. The street where Mr Femi lives is lined with pawn shops and Greek restaurants, peepshows and poolrooms. Hillbrow is buzzing, even this early in the day – muscled men leaning on barstools at the strip club doors, talking to the beautiful girls in their high-heeled boots, smoking cigarettes and waiting. Out on the pavement, hawkers guard their stocks of butternuts and roasted chicken feet. You have to dodge out of the path of a Shangaan maize-seller carrying on her head a brazierful of coals. Black smoke clouds your face, filling your nostrils.

You are still coughing when you step into Bismillah's. Inside, at a window table, Abdoulaye is waiting with Mr Femi. They've been sipping tins of Black Label beer, into each of which, Abdoulaye tells you later, the businessman has dropped two hits of speed.

Mr Femi seems delighted to see you. He towers over you, tall as a preacher in his beautiful grey suit, his sunglasses reflecting your uncertain smile. He orders chicken and rice with a wave of a wrist adorned with a silver Tag Heuer watch. Then, in-between mouthfuls, he explains. A week's paid holiday at a luxury resort, cash for clothing and toiletries before departure, spending money in Sao Paulo, then R30,000 when you get home. Or rather, months and months' worth of rent on a bedsit – a place for you and Abdoulaye and the child, when it comes. Light and air seems to push up between his words, like tiny blessings.

Sipping your Coke, you consider the risks. What you have to remember, Mr Femi keeps saying, is that you are the last kind of person the police will watch for – someone pregnant, someone white. Perhaps this is true. The blacker you are, the more suspect – that's the South African way. When the cops raided Abdoulaye's flats looking for illegals, they'd called them makwerekwere – cockroaches. Anyone whose skin was dark-dark they questioned, and if their victim couldn't count to ten in Afrikaans, they threw him in the back of their van. Abdoulaye pulled off the masquerade perfectly, singing them the words of the song you taught him: Ja, een ding kan jy seker weet, jy gaan jou brood verdien in jou gesig se sweet. One thing's for sure, in this life you earn your dough by the sweat of your brow.

Later, the deal sealed, Mr Femi waves you goodbye with more expansive smiles and you spin back onto the street to find a bus back to Berea. Up in his room, Abdoulaye shields the two of you from prying eyes by propping open the wardrobe beside his bed – a sign to the other men living there not to come near. He plays you a song in French on his guitar. It is about you, he says, your beauty and courage and bravery, and when he gets back to Senegal it will go straight to the top of the hit parade and make you both rich. *Diiyaa niyo, diiyaa niyo*, he whispers to you, and you do it from behind so as not to hurt the baby, and you fall asleep with the smell of the squeezed sap from your bodies on your hands. His or yours, so what – you couldn't care.

You wake to the sound of a siren. Tubes dangle from the shiny white ceiling, swaying as you turn a corner. Your lips, underneath what you realise is an oxygen mask, feel cracked. Your first thought is that you're back on the plane, but then it dawns on you. An ambulance. You're clear of the airport, jirre, you've bloody done it. A man wearing a blue paper mask and blue protective clothing sits on the grey seat beside you. He is reading, with hands that tremble ever so slightly, a TAP in-flight magazine.

Sandro.

There is something very important you have to tell him. Your hands flutter to pull away the mask, but by now he's noticed that your eyes are open and he moves towards you with soothing gestures.

'Michelle, *princesa*,' he is saying, stroking a tangle of blond hair from your face. 'Michelle, you've gone into labour, but you're going to be fine. You're dilating very nicely and ...'

Your voice, forced out with enormous effort, is hoarse. It sounds like somebody else's. 'Asseblief tog, please. I don't want it any more, get it out of me. I don't want it to hurt ... baby.'

But the man is soothing you, telling you in a calm voice not to worry. 'Breathe in deeply, now, Michelle, and relax,' he says. 'After all, you've got something very precious inside you, eh? Something you really don't want to lose.' And bending over you with loving care, he begins fitting the mask back onto your face.

Security

The thief had stood watching us from the upstairs landing. The police worked it all out for us and told us, later. He broke a side window to get into our home, cutting his hand, while outside my mother and I picked leaves from Mrs Xaba's mulberry tree that overhung our lawn. Silkworms were the craze at school that summer and the mulberry leaves were for my shoeboxful, although looking after them was a chore I'd got bored with after only a week. Climbing our narrow stairs, the thief had pressed a bloodied thumb upon the landing window sill as he paused to watch us pick, my mother fluttering her hands amongst the dancing leaves, beseeching me in her anxious voice to stop breaking the tips off that aloe bush and give her a helping hand. Then the thief had rifled through my mother's underwear, emptying over it strings of hair and soiled tissues from the bathroom bin before stuffing her jewellery into a pillowcase and departing as swiftly as he came.

Everybody who came to help was very kind – the two policemen; the gold-toothed detective; the fingerprints guy with his little brush. Yet they all said the same thing: when it came to home security, my mother had been quite astonishingly lax. Never mind that ours was a quiet dorp in the middle of the Klein Karoo, the threat of attack was always lurking: the damage could have been so much worse. An eight-foot-high, multi-zone electric fence was what he had at home, explained the older of the two policemen, shaking his head at our white picket fence over which my mother had trained bougainvillea in a wavering crest. A motion-sensor alarm system and a panic button wired to a rapid-response team, licensed to shoot – that'll keep the skollies out, nodded the fingerprints guy. Put it this way, said the tall, grey-haired salesman who came with a quote for new burglar bars, you had to be on the ball to survive in South Africa nowadays.

My mother listened and nodded, wiping away tears. She wept easily, and apologised often for doing so. Her boy's safety and stability was her life's work, she told the tall salesman in a trembling voice. She had only herself to blame for making such a mess of things. Then she brewed him a cup of coffee, mentioning for the second time my father's death in a car crash when I was only one.

The salesman replied that his name was Pienaar, but that she could call him Pete. He saw what she was up against, he said, inclining his grizzled head towards her and flexing his heavy hands. A woman all on her own, raising a laaitie in a world where it was difficult to know who to trust. And yet it was obvious that she had been trying her best.

Mr Pienaar's voice was deep and strong. I couldn't imagine it ever becoming nervous or wobbly or shrill with unshed tears, or in any way appearing to be afraid. It was a solid voice, as solid-seeming as Mr Pienaar himself.

My mother offered Mr Pienaar another cup of coffee, and after that, a glass of wine. Neighbours – they could also be a problem, Mr Pienaar continued, resenting constructive criticism of their security arrangements and a bit of expert advice. He'd noticed a property not three doors down that was all gone to seed (Billy Niemann's, my mother breathed, gazing at him with shining eyes), which must be a magnet for burglars for miles around. That kind of thing could give even the bravest little householder the jitters, Mr Pienaar said. If it was up to him, he'd chuck the guy who owned it in a jail cell and throw away the key.

By the time my mother hastened me up to bed with a sandwich on a tray, she and Mr Pienaar had almost finished the bottle of wine. 'Your home should be a sanctuary for you and your family,' Mr Pienaar was murmuring, reaching a meaty forefinger towards my mother's small wrist. 'Your home is the only place where you can control who gets close. When it comes to your boy's protection, don't you think only the best should do?'

Within a few hours, my mother had agreed to allow him to draw up a bespoke security plan for her consideration. Within a month, she was bringing up the subject of Mr Pienaar – or Uncle Pete, as she wanted me to call him – moving in. 'You're nearly twelve, you know,' my mother said. 'A boy your age needs some sort of a father figure, really, Boet.' She stroked a curl of hair behind my ear. 'Boet, my sweetheart. Oh, Boet. Maybe it's true I'm just too much of a softie with you, hey?' This is what my mother said in her anxious tones, a week before Uncle Pete arrived with his collection of country music CDs that no one but he should touch, and his big black holdall with the broken zip.

In the beginning, I was an optimist about Uncle Pete. I thought things might improve when he took me hunting at Riet's Drift, or camping by the river at Daggaboersnek. But they didn't improve. I vomited when the first pigeon I shot fell to the ground leaking blood, its beak opening and closing, and Uncle Pete had to wipe everything up, impatiently reporting back to my mother that I must have had a stomach upset. On our camping trip he left me wandering the veld for hours when I got lost going alone to the toilet block in the dark. He reminded me later that he'd explained while he was braaing the meat about navigating by the Southern Cross. He'd thought that a boy my age would already know about these kinds of things.

One weekend soon after the river camp, I went to gather leaves again from the mulberry tree that cast its dappled shade across our lawn. My mother blew me a kiss as she passed: on Saturdays she worked the morning shift at the Bank. I watched the car pull away and turn left down Protea Drive. I whistled a tune. It was a nice day. Hot, the cicadas revving up to full volume, the sky bright as tin.

Inside, amid the cool shadows of the hallway, I disturbed Uncle Pete reading the messages on my phone. His whole body stiffened when he saw me. 'And this is the care you take of your belongings?'

My phone had been missing for about two days. I was always losing it.

He thrust his face closer to mine, the light gleaming off his glasses in a way I didn't like. 'So now, Boet. You told me you looked everywhere for this phone, but just now I find it in the laundry basket. What oke doesn't check thoroughly through places like the laundry basket when he's lost something, hey? Especially when it's a valuable piece of equipment that cost good money to buy?' And he gave me this little klap on the head.

Too late I saw the warning signs, but knew better than to mouth off. Besides, I was alone in the house, with no backup. I kept my eyes down. My stepfather had been speaking in a low monotone, as though relaying a message from somewhere else, but as I stood there, I was filled with bitter resentment against him and the circumstances that brought him to our house. The force of my feeling also shed light on something I had not fully understood before: I hated him. There was no use pretending anything different about it; it was hatred that my stepfather made me feel. Toxic with the knowledge, I snatched the phone from his outstretched hand and ran back out the door.

I had no thought in my head except to seek out something forbidden, to spite my Uncle Pete. Running down the road, I saw that Billy Niemann's truck was gone from his driveway. That was good enough for me. The low branch of an old jacaranda made a snaky springboard across Billy's back wall. I sat on the branch a moment, listening to the faint, persistent ticks and twitches and knockings that jacaranda pods, restless in their warm-air bath, make all day. Everything else was quiet, and that made me quiet too – so quiet that I couldn't move, until the chug of a lawnmower from a few doors down cracked the spell.

Slowly, I sank to the ground. The place was a mess. Tangled grass and weeds choked the flowerbeds. Water seeped from the guttering along the back wall of the house, leaving greenish patches shaped like long-lobed ears. The stoep was a wilderness of litter, rusty garden chairs and an enormous spider plant which had burst its paint-tin pot. Three or four more tins, in some kind of frenzy, had been stomped right in.

In the town Billy was regarded as peculiar. When grown-ups spoke of him, it was always with a special voice and lowered glance, because he had been a bull of a boy once, handsome, with his mother's black curls, and the best prop forward the school coach had ever seen, with lightning acceleration. Every summer at Kelly's Beach, they said, you'd find him battling through the breakers in his lifeguard's cap, towing back to safety a drunk who'd swum out on a dare, a matron with cramp in her slabby calves or a sobbing youngster, twirled away by a sudden current from the deep.

What happened to him was a mystery, people said. His mother was a widow who ran a religious bookshop in the town and subscribed to the old Dutch Reformed Church values; always, at a braaivleis or in the restaurant of the Rhodes Hotel, she'd take nothing stronger than a sip of Coke. When Bill turned eighteen and got his call-up papers, you never saw a woman so proud. She was even prouder when he got sent to Angola because then he'd see actual combat in the Border War. On his first pass home, though, Billy cornered and hurt in an outbuilding the old man who took care of his mother's garden, tying him down first with a coil of wire. His mother paid the man's family off; she took the view, people said, that some foreign virus had temporarily taken hold of her boy's brain.

But then on his next leave Bill took to hanging around the Victoria Girls' High School, pressing on the girls gifts of his own sperm – stored, the story goes, in those small plastic bags banks use to issue coins. After that, his ma could no longer shield him. The mental hospital came with an ambulance, and three thickset orderlies. What funds he had to live on when they finally let him go were from his mother's investments, and when she died (of a broken heart, some said) he scarcely stirred from her house again.

I crept through the tangled undergrowth of Billy's garden and around a tall monkey-puzzle pine, with branches so large and heavy that I had to wriggle flat to pass beneath them.

I inched towards the back door. It was unlocked. The room was almost empty, although there was a blanket on the floor, as if somebody had been sleeping there. The choked hum of a filter motor inside a cloudy fish tank told me that even in the quiet and the dark something near was alive, and I felt a lurch in my stomach, but I didn't move. I sniffed the air – stale tobacco and dirty clothes, cut with something sweetish, like decay – and shivered. In this unkempt, stink-rot place, mad Billy did whatever he wanted, with no grownups to see or hear. The more I thought about it, the more this fact intoxicated me; I imagined Billy driving his seed deep into those bank bags and my hand itched towards my fly. I tried to shift my thoughts away, as if I was a normal, decent person, but deep down I knew I wasn't going to stop my imaginings, and this knowledge made any further delay seem dumb. I jerked down my zip. I kept expecting someone or something to come in and catch me, and the more they didn't, the more excited I became.

Hiding there – hunched over in the dark in a stranger's house, with the sweat springing off me and my mouth all dry – was the best I'd felt for weeks. Everything I felt for my stepfather became an ecstatic force; with every stroke of my hand, that force's power and its righteousness drove my anger home.

Just then my phone started ringing. Scrabbling in my pocket, I seized the traitor by its glowing throat but it skidded through my fingers, bumping up against a shopping trolley filled with old magazines. I heard a door bang then, somewhere very near, and that's when I turned and fled for the garden wall.

Back home, I didn't go indoors straight away. Uncle Pete always bemoaned the fact that the bony toes of our old coral tree made bald patches of his precious lawn, but that morning it was as if those roots had spread themselves there just for me to hide between. After a time, my heart stopped pounding. I could hear my mother clattering about in the kitchen; she had the radio tuned to that Top 40 music station that she liked. I could smell the newly-cut grass.

'I don't believe it,' my ma said. 'Not even a little bit hungry, Boet? You feeling OK?' In her blue summer dress and clean apron she was sitting at the kitchen table, stripping the husks from a pile of yellow mielies.

I shrugged. 'I'm fine,' I lied. I was slumped beside her, chin pressed to my chest and my eyes glued to my knees, but I could feel her looking me over.

I'd spent the afternoon lying on my bed, listening to a fly turning in dreary circles against the windowpane and wondering what to do. Of course I'd be in trouble for losing my phone again. But breaking into Billy's place? Uncle Pete would peel the skin off my arse if he knew. The last time he'd beaten me, it was after he'd spent the whole weekend secretly measuring the bog roll before and after I'd taken a dump, just to prove my extravagant ways with the two-ply. Sometimes that was all it took with him.

My mother leaned over and put her hand on my forehead. Her breath was warm and smelled of strawberries. I wrinkled my forehead to nudge her fingers down a bit. I wanted to save her from the massive, lumpy line of volcano-pimples I'd got lurking underneath my fringe.

She said: 'Doesn't feel like you've got a temperature.' She bit her lip. And then, 'Anything bothering you, my boy?'

'Not really.'

I'd like to have said, I wanted to say: 'I'm scared of getting whipped again, and, by the way, something super-weird happened to me today.' I'd like to have said: 'I did something weird and I never wanted it to stop,' but that would be owning up to beatable behaviour, so I said nothing.

Mom was twisting a pearl ear-stud. She seemed even quieter than usual. The night before, there'd been another row. 'And what gives you the fucking right?' I'd heard Uncle Pete yell. Maybe he thought I was deaf as well as dumb. Now my mom frowned and when I frowned back, she put out her hand again and stroked my cheek. 'My old sweetheart,' she said, her eyes welling up in that way she had, like it was still just the two of us living there. 'My old sweet.'

The new security gate on the back door clanged shut. After a moment, Uncle Pete marched in from the garden, gripping a bundle of leaves. He passed me and as he did, he reached out and, with a finger, flicked me hard on the ear. Just quickly, so my mother didn't see. 'Hey,' he said, loudly. 'How about hopping off your backside, my china, and giving your ma a hand?'

My mom said: 'Ag, he's not feeling so well, Pete. He doesn't even want to eat.'

'Bet you a double Bacardi and Coke he makes it through the night,' Uncle Pete said, with a sniff. 'Think he's got enough strength left to feed the silkworms?'

And he threw down some mulberry leaves from Mrs Xaba's tree. I didn't say anything, but I was very surprised he was bothering to help. He hated anything to do with animals. Often, I'd come home from school and he'd be ranting and bellowing because the Xaba's bantam cockerel wouldn't stop crowing. 'That woman's bird is doing my head in!' Uncle Pete would yell. 'It's getting to be like a bloody farm round here. It's driving me nuts!' I would run and sit in my room upstairs and listen to his loud voice getting louder and my mom going, 'Peter! No!' and then I'd hear the back door slam.

One time after he did this, the cockerel did actually stop and we were both amazed and even scared. What if Uncle Pete had stomped the creature to death, what would happen? 'He'll have to buy her a new one. There's probably something about it in the Constitution,' I told my mom. What I hoped, but didn't say, was that if you murder someone's pet, the kêrels would surely come and take you to jail. But by the time he returned hours later, his tread unsteady and his breath all sour with beer, the cockerel was crowing again.

My mother defended his outbursts, reminding me that when he was just a laaitie the army had sent him to the Border, and what he had gone through there no kid of eighteen should have to bear.

'He never talks about it,' I said.

'He might do, sweet. When the time is right.'

But I just felt tired when she said that. All the white boys at school, their dads had got call-ups to the army and off they went. Those dads sometimes told you stories about getting their hair shaved off and the bad food, and how we were all softies who had it easy – unless it was Liebowitz's pa, who'd been an Objector and gone to jail instead. Yet I'd never heard Uncle Pete talk about that stuff to anyone, least of all to me. He wouldn't give away so much as a clue. I'd think to myself: he doesn't reckon I'm man enough to hear.

And then I'd think: or maybe he's saving his war stories for when the two of them have their own son.

It was hot in the kitchen, so hot you couldn't breathe. Everything was gradually becoming slower and sleepier until suddenly there was the supper table all set, and my mom cutting slices from a soft white loaf. In the violet evening, the lights were coming on along our road. I pictured Billy with my phone, calling the number marked 'Home' and my Uncle Pete answering, and I felt a prickle of cold-sweat dread.

When I opened my eyes again, he was leaning down towards me, his big head with its grey curls right next to my own. He fixed me with his unblinking gaze. 'Welcome back!' he said, smirking at his little joke. 'This is Ground Control, calling occupants of interplanetary craft!'

I gave him a half-smile to show I was playing along, although I didn't feel like smiling. It was just easier that way.

A whole day longer I waited for him to catch me out.

The Sunday afternoon rugby match was in full swing on TV when, almost with relief, I heard his throttled yells change pitch.

I descended the steps quite calmly. 'Ja, Uncle, you called?' I said.

In the big, cool sitting-room that smelt of Cobra floor polish, Uncle Peter in his jogging shorts hugged a beer to his greying chest and glared at the TV screen. 'Phone's gone again, hmm?'

I felt hot all over. 'Sorry?' I said.

'Don't give me grief, my boy – you're not answering your phone!' He took a swig from the can. 'I've sent you four texts since breakfast time. You've lost it again, né?'

'I've been listening to the radio upstairs, I didn't hear it ring.'

'Where is it?'

'Upstairs. Somewhere upstairs.'

'Chomma, don't come now with any of your nonsense. You hear?'

I swallowed. 'I hear you, Uncle.'

'You can twist your mother round your little finger but I am responsible for you as well. You hear?'

'Ja.'

'I can get pushed so far and then that's it.'

By now I was gatvol of the whole game. 'But I was going to tell you …' and I spun him a line about the phone slipping from my pocket as I helped my mother unload shopping from the car. 'You know how the municipality have been so slack about cutting the verges lately,' I added. This was a particular thing with him, but I could hear how wobbly the words sounded, how lame.

He just sat there looking at me. 'OK, then,' he said, evenly. 'We'll find it together. We'll search the whole place until we do. And if we don't find it, I'll beat you. Understand?'

Outside our front gate, a hot wind fanned red grit into the corners of my eyes. 'It's definitely in here somewhere,' I muttered, motioning to the tangle of creeping vegetation outside our house. 'This is the place.' My voice sounded high and childish and with that, time began to speed up tighter and tighter to the moment, not far away now, when I knew his belt would bite the flesh of my back and thighs.

Uncle Pete fetched a panga from the shed and closed in on the verge. He hacked a crazy, zigzag path all the way down to Billy's gate before he spat out a word. 'So where is it, Boet? Was it here you dropped it? Or here? Can you see it yet?' He was still flailing about with the panga, his face dark with a righteous sweat and fury at me and my stupid, lying ways. I could see the spittle stuck in pale beads on his lips. Bits of stick and leaf mould stood out at odd angles in his wiry hair.

Just then there was a cough from a little red car parked against the kerb. From behind his dark glasses Mondi from No. 38 gazed at us impassively, a Marlboro dangling from his bottom lip. Only a year ago I'd watch him pop wheelies down our road, school tie flying. Now he slouched behind the wheel of his Volkswagen as he rode back and forth from the Technikon in the next town over, accompanied, most days, by a diminutive girl who favoured clothes in bright colours worn tight.

'Afternoon, sir,' he nodded. 'Billy's got himself a new gardener, I see?' There was an unruly snigger from the girl in the passenger seat. 'May I say, you're doing an excellent job? Although I think –' he gestured towards a spray of bright pink bougainvillea mottling Billy's wall – 'you may have missed a spot right there. You gotta practise, man! Practise makes perfect, yes?' And Mondi took off his sunglasses and grinned.

I bit my lip. I could hear my stepfather breathing through his nose. I wondered if he might smash the windscreen and drag Mondi through the wreckage by his throat, but at that moment, shouting to her cockerel who scurried before her, Mrs Xaba came panting out onto the street, holding out her broad arms and laughing.

'Hayi, wena, come back here, man!' Large and peaceful-looking, her broad face was topped by a foam of snowy hair. Her calls were not quite drowned by the cheers of three of her grandchildren, racing after her through the garden gate.

Lanky Mondi's efforts to retrieve the bird as it dashed down the road caused all the Xabas to laugh uproariously. The shouting and teasing that followed, in isiXhosa far too fast for me to clutch at, swept us further to the margins until, with the rooster crushed to her majestic chest, and still without heeding Uncle Pete or myself, the old lady turned away.

With a sigh, Uncle Peter lowered his blade. As he did so, the last of the fright in me subsided, cold treachery leaping to take its place. I thought again of Billy's house, and the wild undertow the place had stirred in me. I waited, staring at my stepfather as he failed to speak. I watched as the afternoon sun illuminated the absurdity of a middle-aged man brandishing a panga amid the gates and hedges of a small-town road. He took off his glasses to rub the bridge of his nose, and in that brief, unemphatic motion I glimpsed for the first time the weariness of defeat.

We walked back down the road in an uneasy silence. Half of me still wanted him to roar at my failings – I knew where we stood with that. It led to those moments after the beating when he'd stop, pass a hand over his hair and look at me with such intensity, as if he was trying to remember something. I knew we were close then and despite everything my sore and outraged heart would swell towards him until it almost burst.

On the table in our kitchen, in a pool of late afternoon sun, my silkworms gently rustled in their cardboard box. I stood back as he pulled off the lid and shook out the contents, his face stony as the gleaming creatures, naked bodies quivering, tumbled to the floor. I waited as he stamped the silkworms flat, meticulously, taking his time, until all that was left was a yellow pulp mixed with pieces of broken leaf.

We cleaned up the mess without speaking, I with a mop and bucket, he with a cloth. I was careful to sit in my room for the rest of the evening, and for many days afterwards we kept out of each other's way, as if burdened by a secret each was afraid the other might deny.

My mother and Uncle Pete called it quits not long after that. He left town, found a sales job with a security company on the East Rand, and it seems he never felt the urge to stay in touch.

That was the last we ever saw of uncles in our house. To see my mother after that – like when the ladies from her salsa group came around, all flushed and high from the thrill of it all in the way that Uncle Pete so hated – you wouldn't think a man had ever lived with us at all.

'Boet's been the boss of this house since he was twelve,' my mother tells everyone, proudly. 'He's my rock. Even now, with him all grown up, there's a bond between us that can never be broken, you know?'

I would never tell her how much I still think about Uncle Pete, how even now my thoughts of that sunny afternoon still won't let me rest. Or the way my picture of him gets all mixed up sometimes, and then it's Billy Niemann who comes to trouble me, but the Billy of twenty-five years before, when, as people said, he was a bull of a boy in his prime. And I always seem to see him lithe and golden in his lifesaver's cap, pulling steadily for the shore, and there's a small and shivering form beside him in the water, safely gathered in the harbour of his arms.

Coelacanth

All summer long the car's been sitting there at the front gate. It's not my fault I don't want to drive it. For one thing, it still has my mother's crappy old winter scarf cluttering up the glovebox, and it still smells faintly of her Nicorettes. It just seems weird that I should take over a space that until recently was so intimately hers – it'd be like wearing her pants.

'Give it a clean,' my brother proposes, with a sigh that sounds exasperated, but what about the car's hideous orange colour, like pumpkin soup? Who would pick out a car in such a shade? My mother is a woman of vulgar tastes. My father always joked it was the Afrikaner in her.

'So how will you get yourself down to the beach and back if you refuse to drive that car?' my brother asks, not unreasonably, as we weed the family plot. 'Wheels are freedom. And this summer is supposed to be all about parties and hanging out at Port Kowie with Bibi and all that school's-out-forever fun, right? So what the hell's stopping you?'

The car is my reward for finishing school with respectable marks, although you'd have to be thick not to get the gift's more subtle message: it's time to be moving on. But I don't have time to talk to my brother about the car. I need to talk about a far more shocking and unsubtle piece of treachery on my mother's part, which has sparked something even more complicated in me.

'Her, a boyfriend? Already? Holy crap!' my brother says, with his laugh that's more like a snort, and then: 'Hard, man. Hard as nails. She threw you in the Kowie, remember?' And he starts to tell it all again as we dig and scrape and sweep. Our parents had taken the two of us on a picnic up the estuary to Horseshoe Bend, and my mother was exasperated that at the age of five I was still too scared to paddle off the river banks.

'So you come up, your face like glass with the water streaming off it,' my brother says as he rests his trowel on the rim of our grandfather's grave. 'You look so solemn, you're concentrating really hard to keep afloat – and everything seems to go slow. You go under a second time. Meanwhile we're all just parking off there frozen, looking at the river, and this brak smell of the mud and the milkwoods all about, and I keep on looking, and that's when I can't take it anymore. Never to this day have I held fear like that in my arms, man – pure fear. I get you to the car where it's warm, water dripping everywhere, wrap you in my T-shirt. "She'll survive," is all that Ma will say.'

'But you know her dad threw her in the farm dam when she was also five,' I remind him, as he renews his attack on the hard soil against a headstone where thistles have sprung. 'It's the way kids in her family were taught to swim. Grandpa Bezuidenhout,' I add. 'Him. Right here.'

'Ag, Annie, you've got to make up your mind whose side you're really on. You always defend her, man, and you don't have any reason for it. You need to get the hell out of her clutches,' he says impatiently, and I bite my tongue. It is tedious to hear him repeat the old grudges against my mother, but this is also the last summer before I leave for university, and I'm touched by how it seems to make him want to connect – to shore up our meagre store of family myth before I'm gone.

With my rake I twirl a flounce around the grave of Great-aunt Gezina (born Fort Beaufort, 1945), the dust rising red beneath its prongs. It's borrowed from a family who grow pumpkins over by the high north wall, beneath a marble angel mourning a missing wing. These days the hungry make use of this cemetery without much hindrance.

'Chances are I won't be doing this kind of thing for her when the time comes. Has she ever thought about that, hey?'

My brother uproots an oozing clump of weeds with quick, brusque strokes, tossing them down on the moss I've brushed from the grey headstones. It's beginning to rain.

He is a rational man. But he came back from his post-doctoral stint in the States all changed – quite proud, now, of his preference for men – and our mother finds that hard to take.

'I don't think it ever crosses her mind, and I'm not being funny about it,' I say, uncomfortably. 'You know how she is. When that tyre on the new car blew the other week – it could have been serious, but she never turned a hair. She just puts her head down and avoids the big picture. Maybe she thinks she's immune.'

My brother snorts. 'Maybe you've hit the nail on the head. Maybe mending fences with me isn't an issue for her because she simply reckons she'll outlive us all.' And then our eyes lock, like when we were young, when we competed to see who could go the longest without blinking, although this time I know we're both imagining the same thing – the third row of our plot, stretching behind us with its single, raw grave, the one where our father lies.

The only time my mother lights up a smoke these days is when she's het up. I remember a terrible row she had with a visiting cousin one Easter; she deliberately tripped the switch on our house's lighting circuit and spent the evening huddled on a kitchen chair, invisible save for the lava glow of her cigarette.

Back at home I find her with her hair in curlers. She's slicing lamb's kidneys at the table and there's a Benson and Hedges gripped in the corner of her mouth.

'You look like a drowned rat. Didn't I say to take an umbrella?'

I hold up the pumpkin instead of replying.

'Where did you get that?'

'A man was growing them in the cemetery.'

'It's a disgrace. That's what it's come to now in this country. Everything crumbling to pieces like some Third World joke. Why bring it home? Why encourage such a person?'

'I just wanted to.'

'Don't expect me to cook the horrid thing. You've not forgotten that Bokke is coming tonight?'

The man my mother is seeing is named Bokke du Preez. Like I told my brother, there's no avoiding the fact that they are more than just friends because tonight for the first time he's coming round to the house.

'You'll be off gallivanting with your pals somewhere nice, I expect,' she says.

'Actually, no. I'm free as a bird. I can wait on the two of you hand and foot.'

She hesitates, and I relent a little. 'Don't worry, I'll just pop my head round the door and introduce myself before I head for the pub. Listen, I'll even put on a clean top.'

'The new blouse with the drawstring waist.'

'What?'

'The puffy one – takes off five kilos, at least. And it hides your tattoo. You'll thank me for insisting we got that blouse, rather than see you waste your savings on those ridiculous stiletto shoes.'

A week ago she'd told me, 'You know you don't have to spend the whole summer stuck in this backwater with boring old me.'

'But I like it. And it's our first Christmas together since …'

'Since your dad died. I know. Of course it is. And it's great for me to have you here, you know? But you should be out with youngsters your own age, having fun. You're going to be leading a whole new life soon, Anita, and so am I.'

And it was then, as she stood on a high stool to put away Grandma Bezuidenhout's gravy boat, that in a casual voice she first mentioned the name of Bokke du Preez.

I shut my door on her after that – for the dreary afternoon, and for most of the next morning, too. But my anger with her is never reliable. Soon enough, a strange nostalgia rises to take its place, pushing me out to the secret places where I played as a child – the rusty garage roof, the coral tree where I'd sit, legs dangling, feeling the sun-warmed bark mould itself to my thighs. Soon enough, it propels me back to my mother to petition her for chores, polishing her antique wedding bracelet with its heavy silver links, suppressing the boredom of doing things that soon there will be no need to do.

Yet for all that, I am not quite back to rights. Something pulls at me, something to do with the wide, electric world out there – it pulls at me with sparkly ideas that prickle and crest, and the more I chase them away, the more they come back to stay. At night, I stare out of my window instead of going to sleep; I stay for hours like that, bathing in the silvery light that drifts between our street and the valley beyond, until a speeding car sends sound waves crashing, sweeping me back down inside my everyday life.

The next morning, Bibi calls me to say she's been down at her parents' beach house at Port Kowie for like seven hours and already she's totally overdone the sun and her nose is this weird like, *umber* shade and it's a complete nightmare. She says there's a party at the Reiners' at the weekend and what is the plan? She says to bring any music I can lay my hands on when I come down, she left a kitbag full of CDs behind. I tell her my mother probably needs me here this weekend, she needs me at home a little longer. The whole bereavement thing – you know. The thing is, Bibi, I say. It might take a while before I can be on my way.

Bokke du Preez is a tall old man who manages a tyre repair shop on Somerset Road. He has an old man's habit of shrugging, 'Ag, nee, wat.' The shrug seems to be his way of admitting defeat. 'What can a poor bloke do?' He looks at my mother sideways and smiles sheepishly, with his hand before his mouth – shielding himself, perhaps, from the blaze of her vitality.

'Hell, but that's a moer of a tjap you've got on your arm there, my girl,' he says to me, but we are not the kind of family that sprinkles Afrikaans words over speech like pepper and salt. My father always preferred his English pure and proper – 'pickup truck', 'Grandpa', 'Goodness, but that's a very interesting tattoo, my girl'. I rake my eyes over to my mother, but she looks away.

Yet Bokke du Preez has come prepared to forge links with the young. He fumbles in his blazer pocket and produces a creased photograph of a tow-headed boy, squinting beside a mighty fish. Bokke's moment of glory, it turns out, came some forty years ago when he spotted a rare specimen of marine life down on the Port Kowie docks.

'Bright blue, with these big, fat fins, man – sticking out like paws. You wouldn't believe it. Just lying there under a heap of rays and sharks and some other rubbish in the trawler boat nets.'

Like most children of this little town, Bokke du Preez had seen our natural history museum's prized coelacanth specimen – that many-finned fish of ancient lineage – on no less than three separate school trips, so he knew what to do. 'I tell my old man to give the fisherman a few bob. At first the oke doesn't want to sell, but then my dad starts asking questions about his operating licence, stuff like that – he soon changes his mind. You should have seen the faces of the people at the museum when we rock up with this five-foot-long freak, wrapped up in pages from my dad's *Scope* magazine!'

'Don't waste your breath telling her that story,' my mother interjects. 'Anita will freak out. When the school took her class to see the coelacanth, it gave her nightmares for months. Years, actually. Drove me crazy. Hair-trigger imagination, this child.'

My mother is on edge tonight. She has changed out of her usual T-shirt and jeans into a kind of leather pants affair with a sparkly top. Her lipstick is red. It does not suit her.

'How much did you get for the fish?' I ask.

'Ag, it was getting vrot by the time we got to the museum – they didn't want to know. My dad, you check – he'd made me sit in the car for the whole afternoon, waiting, while he parked off with the coelacanth in the Cathcart Arms. He wanted to show it off to his pals, but in that heat ...' He shakes his head.

Outside, the rain casts the shadow of a thousand blue scales across the glass.

'What a thing, though, man,' Bokke du Preez says. 'Hell of a thing.' For a moment, he sounds grave and fearless, like a TV announcer, instead of a sheepish old man.

He puts the picture away carefully in his blazer pocket and pauses, his eyes suddenly blank behind his spectacles, until my mother declares, smiling at him in her new, triumphant way, that supper is almost ready and what about another cold beer before the two of them sit down to eat?

The hotel bar where I spend the evening stands on an old road that's wide enough to turn an ox-wagon. Inside, I shoot pool with a travelling salesman from Kokstad who smells of whisky and stale sweat. I stay until closing time, then I walk home. The rain has stopped and there is no traffic on the street. I'm standing outside the gate, listening to the night sounds, when I see a man in our garden relieving himself against the hedge. The stream is long, and spatters on the grass. Shaking himself clear, catching the last drop on a pale thumb-tip which he puts meditatively into his mouth, Bokke du Preez tips his big head back to snuff the midnight air. Then, finally, he stuffs the long, white cock back inside his pants.

That night, the dark gives way to a terrible dawn – crimson, fading to coral in the east – which shocks me rigid, because it lasts for days. The whole street is affected, every window glowing warm to the touch. The air is quite stagnant beneath this strange, meaty sky, and my throat feels full of dust. There is no other light, no birdcalls; not a twig stirs.

The next morning, his car is gone, although I am pretty sure I lay awake most of the night and never heard it leave.

'Have a good evening?' I ask.

My mother is vacuuming the dining room and humming a little tune. The rain has stopped. Through the open French doors I can see the papery late roses basking under a pale sun.

'Come on, then, let's get it over with,' she says. 'Tell me your opinion of him. I'm in a hurry to get to the supermarket to do inkopies.'

I am wary of this language. 'Inkopies' is not part of our family vocabulary.

'I am ready,' my mother says coldly, and she looks hard and cold and unflinching, her lips shut.

'Well, I don't know … he seems an OK sort of a chap. Hardly an intellectual giant, I guess. What will the ladies in your bridge club make of him?'

With a sudden grating aggression in her voice she snaps: 'You always have some criticism. You never give me any support. If you knew how awful it is to be surrounded by children who are selfish. If your father was here now …'

'His sweet body resting on the bottom of the grave …'

'What?'

Rigid, as if her spine's filling up with iron filings.

'Oh, just a line from a blues song I was listening to. One of Dad's CDs.'

'You're *singing* at me now? Come back here!' my mother shrieks, as I inch out the French doors. The force of her voice swings me back into the room just in time to see her smash the vacuum cleaner to the floor.

'What makes you think you're so bloody special?'

I slam the doors and lean beside them, hushed and waiting; the walls of the house like waves her puny words must swim against.

'I'm sick to death of you,' she screams.

I skip down the path and out through the gate.

'Ja, he's a charmer, alright, a real arsehole.'

I'm lying in bed, almost asleep when my brother calls. His boyfriend had been invited to an office get-together in the Cathcart Arms. Caspar's just sitting at the bar, my brother says, when he notices Bokke du Preez and his friends drinking nearby.

'Quite the centre of attention, Caspar said. They were buying him drinks and getting very fruity about the rich widow their man had hooked. They mentioned her by name, Anita. They were that drunk, Caspar reckoned they'd been sitting in there all afternoon.'

I bury my head under the pillow, and almost drop the phone. 'The thing is,' I finally manage. 'Look. I cannot believe that she sees anything in this weird old loser. But there's nothing we can do. You know what she's like.'

Even when he's on the other end of a telephone, my brother's impatience – so like my mother's – sparks through me like a wire.

'You've got to do something, Anita! Just talk to her, for God's sake. I mean, this is our mother. Our reputation. You know?'

I don't dare tell him that there is something more fiercely triumphant than ever in our mother's manner right now and it cannot be dented. I don't dare tell him, even though this very evening, she'd made an arrangement with Bokke du Preez to go to the movies and he never arrived.

The following morning a text message comes, tersely explaining the circumstances in which Bokke had been called away to Bathurst to road-test a truck. My mother just smiles at me in a more triumphant manner still. The look on her face tells me she is more certain than ever now that he is a man of his word.

'You see? And now he's inviting me to lunch at the Settler's Inn.'

'Ah, the Inn. Bibi's mother went there a while back and got food poisoning. She thinks it was the steak.'

But she returns far too early from the lunch, agitated. 'He called at the last minute,' she says, with a sigh. 'Some problem with work. He's run off his feet in that place, you know.'

I take a deep breath.

'Do you really think this is worth the hassle? Can you really put up with this kind of behaviour?'

'I do. I can. Somehow, he makes me feel young again. It may be crazy of me to say this so soon, but I do think there's something there.'

'What are you going to do?'

'I'll invite him round for dinner again,' says my mother. 'That seems to be the only way.'

The night that Bokke is due to return, I leave the house early. I walk across town to my brother's place and we eat braaied meat. We drink beer, then tequila shots. Finally, my brother starts rolling joints. Caspar puts on Dollar Brand, John Coltrane, Abba's 'Waterloo'. We drink more beer.

By the time I am ready to attempt the long walk home, it is starting to get light.

I find my mother seated in her leather pants and high heels at the kitchen table. She doesn't turn to look at me, or speak. She just sits there, staring at the leaves that wave through the half-open window, wrinkled as finger ends. We stay like that for a while. Then, gripping the table edge, my mother rises. She walks right past me and begins to scrape uneaten food from a casserole dish into the bin.

Frozen in the doorway, I hear a muffled sound. It's been a long time since I heard her cry, so long that the memory almost seems like something out of a fairy tale.

'You never give me enough support,' I had heard her sob. 'I know she twists you round her little finger, but what about me? What about me?'

My father comforted her. 'It's not your fault,' he soothed. 'She has an over-active imagination, that's all. Go back to bed. I'll deal with the nightmares from now on.'

Listening from my narrow bed, the warm patch beneath me slowly turning cold, it wasn't only wet sheets that were the problem. It was not being able to stop myself demanding her attention – more than she could give, despite knowing that she hated, even feared, the exhausting tug on her energies.

Slowly, I make my way down the corridor, past my father's study with its dusty cheese plant and the old magazines slumbering in forgotten crates. Inside my room, I lie down once again on the bed with the candlewick quilt.

That sense of her as stronger. Of me needing, always lacking that strength – that was the weakness. The thing I could not overcome.

When I was five, my schoolmates and I were taken to the town museum to see the coelacanth, a fish everyone thought had gone extinct in the age of the dinosaurs, but had all along been thriving in the deep waters off the coast near our town. Our teachers stood at the back. In the middle of a hall, in a beam of yellow light, a monstrous creature swung open its jaws. We gaped in shock; we caught at each other's hands. Then, gradually, though the sweat pricked us in strange places and our heartbeats clip-clopped, our collective fright died down. The monster faded – only a fish, after all, entombed in a coffin of glass; boldly we gazed upon its pulpy fins, its flaking papyrus flesh.

But for me a sense of fear beyond the bounds of sense persisted, and that's when the dream began. Even now there is a memory, stirring ghostly fronds in the secret gullies of my brain. Nothing changes, the water monster says to me: I have been here forever and I will always be the stronger one, biding my time in the cradling dark. Thrash and kick all you might to get away, but you will never escape, falling, failing, falling down through my domain to the eddying numbness below – to the things unseen, and the wormy sand.

Over the years, the nightmare had sometimes receded for patches of time, but it always came back, eating up the will to start a separate life.

Remembering it now, and the stooped and quivering shoulders of the suddenly old woman in the kitchen, I feel a sense of urgency that has no understanding in it. I stare up at the ceiling a moment longer. And then, hearing my mother shifting on her kitchen chair, I get up and drag my bags out from under the bed.

I make no effort to hide what I am doing. When I have finished packing, I tidy the bed and smooth the quilt back into its proper place.

Before I leave, I glance out across the garden towards the street. The sweetness of the dark plums shaken out of the old grey tree; red seed glinting in the black soil beneath the coral tree; morning sun coming and going through the big clouds sweeping in from the valley. Everything so dearly familiar to me, and I to it. Outside our gate, I see a scattering of new petals have fallen on the grass. The white Cape Chestnut has come into bloom; the pink will not be far behind.

I climb into the warmth of my car and drive south as quickly as I can, towards the sea.

Home

*They change their sky, not their soul, who rush
across the sea.*

— Horace

They left the flat around four. Far too late to bag the best camping
spot, but then the downpour had kept Sam and her sister trapped
indoors for most of the afternoon. From the dank mouth of the
Mandarin Gardens underpass, the two women walked out into a
clear greenish light that washed in all directions across the deserted
shore. The waves in the Straits were hushed; the water was almost flat
calm. Beneath the sea almond trees, the monsoon had brought out
a smell of rotting loam, the old jungle underlay of urban Singapore.
The city was behind them now.

Out here, she would squeeze a confession from her sister, thought
Sam. Maybe it was just a case of forcing her out of the flat. Nina had
arrived from Johannesburg three days ago, jetlagged and crotchety,
and since then she had hardly spoken, let alone set a foot out of doors.
She just stayed slumped in the spare room, rising every afternoon to
complain about her exhaustion, the humidity, the heat. She would
spend hours in the shower, clogging the drain with long, blond hair
and on more than one occasion, stubbing her cigarette out in the

soap. At night, Nina filled the flat with restless movement as Sam lay listening, so rigid with fury and resentment that she, too, couldn't sleep, imagining her sister touching everything – the red Chinese wedding cabinet, picked up for a song at Expat Auctions, the silly *Singapore is a Fine City* fridge magnet she'd forgotten to hide away. And while Sam had filled the freezer with special dishes that flaunted her newfound familiarity with coconut milk and chilli paste, her sister didn't want any of it. She just lay on her unmade bed munching toast, gazing out at the back side of next door's condo, a glaring tower block of hard, white stone.

In this respect, the two of them had slipped straight back into the roles they'd played as children, with Sam locked in unwilling orbit around Nina's indifferent sun. And yet it had been decades. Twenty-five years since her escape, exchanging home for places where Nina had no pull. Law school in Cape Town, the London scholarship, first steps on the ladder at Wendell Ogilvie, old Mr Cheadle in the international department taking her under his raptor's wing. Reading briefs on the exercise bike late at night, the 6am protein shake, the windowless conference rooms, the weekend drudgery. She'd earned her Singapore secondment, she'd paid her dues. How dismal it always was to find that despite everything, the orbital laws governing her and Nina's tiny constellation still held sway.

Of course, her sister was trapped in her own time warp, too. Their father's behaviour last week had been so cruel – crushingly so, but Nina, ever the daddy's girl, hadn't thought to take Sam's side. Instead, in Changi Airport arrivals hall, she had tried, characteristically, to shrug the problem away. 'Look, there's no easy way to say it, Sammy, but he refused to get on the flight,' she said, avoiding her sister's stricken gaze. 'I went to pick him up at home and it was pretty weird; I mean, I could see his luggage packed and waiting in the hall. But he wouldn't budge – you know how clammed-up he gets when he's cross. I was so worried for him: with his blood pressure he mustn't get stressed, and of course it was all just a nightmare for me, the taxi sitting waiting there in Dad's driveway and the time ticking away and all.' How hard she had really tried to make their father pick up his bags and come to Singapore, how skilfully she had prosecuted her case, Sam didn't know.

The annual family reunion on the anniversary of her mom's death, and the first in Sam's new home out East. That's what the plan had been, and now her father had not come. He was punishing her, simple as that – a situation she would have to endure like the Great Trials of old when, after the sting of the tomato cane on her bare flesh, there'd come a banishment to the dusty waste ground behind the peach trees for only he knew how long.

Why hadn't he come? Perhaps offering to pay for his ticket had been her crime, though Nina disagreed about that. Perhaps it was simply that she'd had the audacity to invite him. After all, it was she who had declared war on their father all those years ago, and now it was she tossing the old man a truce.

But Nina knew the secret reason. Of course she did; she and Dad were inseparable. Out here, with no spare room for Nina to hide in, Sam reckoned she'd prise it out of her and then the holiday could be history, a mistake time would wipe away like bleach on a stain.

In the meantime, she'd be damned if she'd let her sister find any grounds for complaint. Let there be only 'see-what-you-missed' stories for her to take home in that hideous leopard-print luggage set. Let there be no more complaints about jetlag, or bird noise: this morning, she'd ripped the mynah's nest out from underneath the air conditioner that was wedged above Nina's bed. Balanced on the back of her rattan planter's chair, she probed a coat hanger deep beneath the unit's grimy frame, dislodging twigs and feathers, leaves and fragments of fresh shell. She squirted Clorox and scrubbed the spattered window sill, the bitter smell lodging deep in the throat of her day. The parent birds – perhaps disoriented – had come back a few times to perch on the sill; the whole thing had left her vaguely uneasy although she supposed they would all get used to it.

The tent and sleeping bags were heavy, but the effort of carrying them gave Sam and Nina an excuse not to speak. Sam led the way down the East Coast Park's paved track, feeling sweat prickle her scalp after only a few steps. From the big banyan tree by the turtle pond they headed past the hawker centre with its seafood stalls. It was livelier there, charcoal braziers sizzling, families gossiping over plates piled with grilled stingray sambal and pepper crab. After twenty lukewarm British summers, how good it felt to be back amongst the body language of hot weather people, where you knew that the man caressing his hairy back with those long, slow scratches was the victim of a mosquito's vampire kiss; where even the kids ambled slow as pensioners, trying to dodge the pulverising effects of the sun.

They still had a way to go, past the Rent-a-Bike hut, past Bedok Jetty and the crowded campsite there, to the quieter, grassy stretch Sam liked beneath the pines. A high-risk strategy, this, persuading the Queen of the Suburbs to come camping – even to a park as manicured as this. Yet Nina had not resisted, much. 'Time to focus, I guess,' she'd said, yawning. 'Remember those camping trips up the Sundays River with Dad when we were small? And you're right – would be a pity to waste the permit, especially now I know, because you've told me three bloody times, that you queued for an hour for it in the heat.'

This reunion had not even been her idea, but Nina's. Nina had all the time in the world for planning; she sat in that big house on the hill with nothing to do except think up ways to spend her divorce settlement and hang out with her friends at the gym. She wondered, not for the first time, whether Nina would ever go back to work. She'd spent years as Nick's PA, helping him build up his IT business from scratch. But perhaps being married to the company boss had been the only motivating factor where Nina's career was concerned, and both those roles were done with, now. Blood ties or no, she'd never been able to work out what made her sister tick, not really.

Nina had said: 'Dad and I are tired of trying to tempt you back for a visit, even for a week.' She had given a dry laugh. 'How long has it been now since you were back in South Africa – twenty years?' What Sam still considered a flight for survival, Nina just found baffling. She would say that their father was old now, that it was time to forgive his inadequacies as a single parent all those years ago, that it meant a lot to him, the London visits to see Sam – that it would mean so much more if she could just pay a single visit home. In life, you only got one father, and theirs had made many sacrifices so that his two girls might succeed. Of beatings and banishments, endless stand-up rows, the declarations that he could not support a left-winger, a kaffir-boetie, she would say, I survived those things, so can you. Sam would think, no, you didn't.

This time, Nina had changed tack. 'Can you fit us both into the Singapore flat?' She was hunched on a chair, painting her toenails as they spoke on Skype. The yellow mug at her side, Sam knew, would be full of rooibos tea. 'Dad's really keen to see your new spot. And as I keep telling him, I think it would be so special if he came out to see you this year of all years.'

'Are you nuts?'

'No, listen. There's a 70th anniversary gig going on with the POW support group, you know? He's been sent all sorts of emails inviting him to things.' Their father had been evacuated from Singapore at the age of five, one of the lucky ones. His own father, a mining engineer working in Malaya, had been taken prisoner by the Japanese, dying of dysentery in Syme Road internment camp after just six weeks.

'… Sammy? And he wants to see you too, of course. Look, Sam. Look. Only for a week. I'll be there as well, alright? I'll help with everything. Two years since the last meet-up. Water under the bridge now. Look, I really do think it'll work out better this time.'

'At least it'll be sunny, I suppose.'

'What?'

'If there is the usual huge bust-up, at least it'll be sunny. Makes a difference. Not like that terrible time in Holborn, remember? The row over how rude he was to the waiter. Dad stomping off and getting lost on the Underground, ending up frozen half to death in the snow in Rayner's Lane.'

'Yes, well, that's exactly it. We're coming to check out the new, sunny Sam. We're done with the buttoned-up version, freezing us out with British reserve. What we want now is the Zen reinvention. Chilled out, relaxed from eating top-grade sushi and meditating on top of a tower block. Like a … ja, like a little Taoist monk.'

'You know what, Neens? One of the joys of being a perpetual foreigner is that it forces you to see with fresh eyes all the time. Keeps you from getting stale, from relying on the cheap stereotype, you know? I recommend it.'

'Doesn't it make you scared, though?'

'What?'

'Scared of dying in some foreign place, talking away in broken Afrikaans like a stuck record that no one understands.'

'Jesus, Nina. Charming. I'm only bloody forty-two.'

'Anyway. So you'd be up for it, then? For a couple of weeks at Christmas time?' Nina took a small sip from the yellow mug.

'I'm up for it, but … can any good come of it, Neens? I'm really not sure.'

'Worth a try, Sam. It's definitely worth a try. Bloody brilliant! Look, I know how you like to obsess over the details, but just relax about this and leave everything up to me, OK? Let me handle it. You'll see.'

Sam had opened a fresh legal pad and jotted down the visiting hours at Changi War Museum and the soldiers' cemetery at Kranji. She bought new bed linen and put down an eye-wateringly large deposit for Christmas lunch at Raffles Hotel. Beside her father's bed in the yellow spare room she laid down, then took away again, a copy of the *Straits Times* article that called her law firm 'a star of Singapore's growing International Arbitration scene'. She hoped it would all be enough. She expected to detect the usual resentment in her father's manner towards her work-focused way of life, but she also knew that Nina would be watching, poised to smooth over the cracks. Their father was her sister's guiding light, and she in turn was alert to his every whim. Back home in Port Elizabeth they lived only a mile apart, braided into each other's lives: shopping trips, cream teas at Apron Strings, the cinema. When Nina spoke to Sam on Skype she complained incessantly of his demands, yet without rancour. It was complete nonsense, of course – a crippling dependency on both their parts, yet it seemed to make them happy.

'You're well kitted out, aren't you, Sis?' Now Sam wondered for the thousandth time, as they shook the tent from its bag and cleared a space beneath the largest pine, if Nina had really said anything positive at all to make the old man get in that airport car.

'What? Yes – the camping gear belongs to Pearl. My neighbour's maid. You talk about reinventing myself from the top of my tower block? She's been here fifteen years, she wrote the book on all that.'

'She's a maid and she goes camping?'

'Yes, why not? She goes camping because it calms her down. She's putting her daughter back home in Manila through a beauty course and her son through rehab for gambling addiction and she thinks she might be getting the sack soon because Mr Eric, her Canadian boss, just lost his job.'

'How very careless of him. But if Pearl's so stressed out, how come she's not here herself?'

'She's steering clear of the East Coast Park for a week or two. Seems she's been running a card game down here on the weekends, trying to make a bit of extra cash. Luckily, the park ranger who busted her said she reminded him of his girlfriend back in Malacca, so he'd look the other way just this once.'

Tough, resourceful Pearl. In this city of uprooted souls, so nimble-footed; always so sure of her place.

'You talk as if you admire these people. These … cheats.'

Sam didn't say anything. Pointless to try and make Nina understand. Part of the delicious freefall of being not-from-here – estranged from where you lived as well as from the place where you were born – was how it fine-tuned your senses to the unfamiliar. Lawlessness bubbled everywhere in this straight-laced place, if you knew where to look. Even this scrap of a park was a frontier. From Malaysia and Indonesia, just a skip across the Straits, came smugglers in the night with crates of tiger penises and black bear gall bladders, sex charms savagely harvested. Sometimes, the cargo was human, refugees from China risking prison for the chance to scoop a mouthful from Singapore's overflowing rice bowl.

For Nina, though, knowledge of such things was dangerous, and proof of the folly of straying too far from home. Now, digging in the last tent peg, she sat back primly on her heels, taking care not to get sand on her white crocheted top. 'It'll be dark soon,' she said, and shivered. 'You remembered to pack a torch, Sis?' She stood up, dusted off her hands and began to rummage in her backpack for her cigarettes.

'Well, isn't this nice.'

From her seat at the campsite picnic table, Nina turned to Sam with a small, tight smile. They were eating takeaway prawn noodles from the hawker centre and drinking bottles of Tiger beer.

'Uh-huh. Galaxies away from Port Elizabeth, hey? Or rather, Port Elizabeth feels galaxies away from here.'

'Huh, and you're the one who's always ticking Dad off for being politically incorrect. I would have thought you would know that Port Elizabeth doesn't exist any more. He and I live in iBhayi now. iBhayi, in Nelson Mandela Bay.'

Combative as always, just like him. Sam stared at the sea. At dusk, the damp air took on brash colours here, violets and yellows and clashing pinks. Soon the moon would thrust itself above the line of container ships and tankers queueing for the port.

'So what do you think is the real reason Dad didn't want to come out?' Her voice had only the smallest hint of tremor in it, but Nina heard.

'He's very proud of you, Sam. He's been telling everyone about your promotion.'

'So why couldn't he tell me in person?'

'I don't know.'

'You do know.'

'How could I? I don't know what to say to either of you anymore. This thing between you and him? It's boring, you're so stuck it makes no sense, it leaves no room for anything else or anyone else. And you know why it drags on and on? Because the two of you are so much alike.'

'That's nonsense. And you know it. We were never close. Not really.'

The first time she left home without him was on a geography field trip to Mossel Bay. She bought a postcard when the bus stopped at a filling station. 'Dear Dad,' she wrote. 'It's beautiful here, you would love it. I am looking at a flickering campfire as I write. Guess what! Found the Southern Cross like you showed me, Miss Finnegan gave me a merit for showing the class. I've been writing a poem, it starts: The winds quiet song tells a peaceful story and the waves also. Wish you were here. Love Sammy.' Ten days later, back at home with him, an envelope arrived, addressed to her in his familiar hard, spiky hand. It contained her postcard, corrected in red; an apostrophe for 'wind's' and another for 'wave's'. At the bottom he had written: DETAILS COUNT.

As if Sam's silence encouraged her, Nina said: 'He took it personally, you know, you moving out here.'

'But I'm head of department here. It's a fucking promotion!'

'I know. But it was hard. I think you being in London felt more manageable somehow, it's still in the West. I know it's absurd in this age of Skype and round-the-clock flights. But he was like someone defeated when he heard the news. Defeated and old.'

'He's just going to have to handle it, then, isn't he?'

'Of course he'll have to handle it. I think he just felt like you were flying even further away, that's all.'

Unfair, manipulative and just plain wrong. In fact, there was plenty here to remind a South African of home. The skin-whitening creams on sale in every department store. The way the darkest workers – here, Bangladeshi migrants – did all the dirty jobs. And those millionaire Cabinet ministers whose murky family fortunes no one dared probe? Singapore was built from the same crooked timbers as her own country; that case could be quickly made. She smiled, picturing the argument, already seeing the annoyance on her father's face.

'Maybe it's my own fault, Sam. Maybe it was too much to ask, pushing him to come to Singapore, of all places, after all this time. Him not coming may not revolve entirely around you – ever think of that?'

When the bombs started falling on Singapore, their grandmother had taken her small son down to Keppel Harbour and begged berths back to Cape Town on a Dutch mail ship. The SS *Plancius* had stopped off along the way at Batavia and Bombay, two more places that no longer existed.

Not revolve around you. The relief she felt at Nina's words sank down inside her, a shaft of sunlight on a jungle floor. But then force of habit made her blunder on.

'Ja, so nothing in life stays the same, Nina. Things change. And Dad of all people should know that.'

'Oh, Sam, please just stop hating him, alright? Enough! Enough with this stupid game!' Her beer bottle slammed down on the stone table with a dull, unechoing thud.

She did not like to hear that note in her sister's voice. It sounded like Nina's own pain, not the relayed echo of their father's.

A snail, a great dollop of a thing, was oozing down the table leg in the gloomy light. The dark shape moved slowly, almost too slowly for Sam to register any movement, but she watched until it reached the bottom and disappeared into the sweating mulch below. Then, reluctantly, she reached out across the table and took her sister's hand.

'Sam. You awake?'

'Well, I am now. What is it?'

'Sam. This tent is very … hot. Bloody hard on the back, and *hot.*'

'Ag, Neens. So next time, I'll move to Alaska. Sorry, hey? Just try and go back to sleep.'

'Sam. *Sam!*'

'What the hell?'

'Didn't you hear it? That weird noise, just close by?'

'Neens, there's nothing, honest. Just some little tropical frog with a big, weird voice, probably. Don't even think about it. It's all quite safe.'

'No, it was … it was a really strange booming sound all of a sudden. Maybe one of the ships out there was moving or something? I can't believe you didn't hear.'

'They drove the sea away from here, you know. Years ago.'

'What?'

'The Japanese. Some war debt thing. They paid for contractors to come and lop the tops off all the little hills round here and tip it all into the sea. They made a whole new shoreline. Where we're sleeping was ocean floor.'

'Sam. Do you remember the time I got you into such trouble, when we spied on Mom and Dad in the bath?'

Memories surging back like murmurings of water, always looking for their chance.

'I haven't thought about that … Phew! More than forty years, Nina. But it was only Mom who was in the bath. Dad was at the basin, having a shave.'

'It must have been before she got sick, because I remember she still had all her hair.'

'Tell me about it. I was terrified. I'd never seen pubic hair before and there was Mom with that huge seventies bush, all waving tendrils like a Jules Verne sea creature.'

'Ja, and then I fell backwards off the wheelbarrow, and Dad heard, and saw you peeping through the window …'

'And came roaring out to give me the thrashing of my life. Still wearing only his towel. You were nowhere to be seen, and of course he would never believe that it was all your idea.'

'Mmm. Sorry about that, li'l sis.'

'Ja. Well.'

'Sam. So. You … seeing anyone right now?'

'Well, you know. You get to our age and all the good ones are already taken, hey, Neens? There was this one guy, though. Few months back, when I first arrived. You would have liked him. Ben.'

'Oh, yes? Another lawyer?'

'No way. I'm so done with lawyers. A chef. American. Managed this little Mexican place. Great cook, obviously. Liked exploring the heartland neighbourhoods, tracking down the best dishes at the traditional hawker stalls. Liked movies, too. Knows more about Fellini than the man himself.'

'Huh. And so?'

'Ah. Well. So he went off.'

'Putrefaction set in?'

'Ha bloody ha. No. Thai waiter from his restaurant. Some boy half his age.'

'Oh, Sammy. Oh, my.'

'That you laughing, Neens?'

'No! No way. No no. Not at all. But …'

'Ja. Like a bloody soap opera, my love life. Well, anyway. I prefer it this way, I think. Probably. Keeping it all provisional, no ties. But listen, Neens. I was thinking. Why don't we … why don't we take a little trip?'

'You mean next week?'

'Ja, just quick and easy. Just take a ferry somewhere up the Malaysian coast, find a beach shack place on an island. Hang out, chill. Talk.'

'Well, I didn't think you'd ever want me along on … that would be great, Sam. My. How free and easy your life has become. Just swinging off to some tropical paradise whenever you feel you can't face the daily grind. Keeping it all provisional, as you say. Or how about a jungle trek? Something to tell the girls at the gym, you know?'

'Possibly, Neens. Possibly. My friend Victoria found a leech on her labia once, after doing a jungle trek. You ready for that?'

'Sheesh, Sam! Heavens! No way, shut up!'

'Well, then.'

'Well, then. We'll make some plans, that's fantastic!'

'OK, then.'

'OK. Hey. You ever coming home, Sammy?'

'No, never. Now go to sleep.'

Nina was snoring gently when Sam woke up in the night. Her watch said one fifteen, but she could hear daytime noises: a ringing cellphone, a badly tuned radio blaring K-Pop, people shouting and laughing. She pulled her shorts on over her T-shirt and slipped out into a blurry shock of shadowy figures and shapes: while she and Nina slept, tents had mushroomed all around. At the stone picnic table, a group of men in stained chef's jackets passed a bottle around; a kind of brotherhood. One of them, an older man thin and dried up as a vanilla pod, turned and shouted something after her as she went past, something in Hokkien that she didn't understand. Behind the group's silhouette, a dim shroud of visibility lit by the glow of the tankers out at sea, the world fell away into darkness. The campsite had become an unknown place.

Crossing the bike track, she watched as a bent old lady in baggy green trousers cycled slowly past. She stared at Sam as if trying to categorise her, uncertain, perhaps, because of unfamiliar details, whether to envy or to scorn. Singapore was loudly acknowledging her foreignness tonight, over-delivering, even, on her need to stand on the outside looking in. In the acid light of the toilet block, a thin woman in high heels screamed at a weeping little boy, slapping his cheek before turning back to the mirror to comb her long, dark hair. Life had first smacked her father in the face when he was about that big, down at Keppel Harbour. Ever since Sam had known him, he had returned the favour by responding in kind and then withdrawing behind silences thick as fortress walls. A harsh challenge she had issued him, to come back to Singapore.

Show him the night sky. That's what she would have done, the first evening he arrived. Far up there, the Southern Cross was aiming his glittering pointer through the darkness, like he does in some hot countries. She and Dad shared the same skies now – the same viewpoint, if you looked at it a certain way. He would have liked it if she'd said that to him. But tonight there was nothing to see but cloud. It was monsoon season. December was different, here, and she had missed her chance with him again.

As she approached the campsite, she realised that she had no recollection of where her sister lay in the dark. All the little humps of nylon with their square mesh windows looked identical to her. Slowly, then with mounting panic, she zigzagged through the maze of tents, hoping to see some familiar feature that would tell her she was home.

Acknowledgements

Many people have had an input into this book but special thanks are due to Russell Celyn Jones, Lucy Roeber, Elizabeth Sarkany and James Whyle for their insightful criticisms and good advice. Thanks, too, to Rosemary van Wyk Smith for early pushings and proddings. I am immensely grateful to Suchen Christine Lim for her generosity and encouragement in matters literary and beyond. Thanks to Colleen Higgs at Modjaji for her faith in the project, my editor, Andie Miller, whose smart and sensitive notes made this book much better than it was, and Carl Becker, for the beautiful cover illustration. Above all, I'm indebted to my husband Mac, who knows the real truth behind the fictions.

For more about Modjaji Books and any of our titles go to
www.modjajibooks.co.za